# Kate

# Kate

by

## Jean Little

HarperCollins*Publishers*Ltd

First published in the U.S. by HarperCollins Publishers and
in Canada by Fitzhenry & Whiteside: 1971
First HarperCollins Publishers Ltd Canadian edition: 1995

Canadian Cataloguing in Publication Data

Little, Jean, 1932-
  Kate

1st HarperCollins Canadian ed.
ISBN 0-00-648073-X

I. Title.

PS8523.I77K3 1995   jC813'.54   C95-931703-1
PZ7.L57Ka 1995

96 97 98 99 ❖ OPM 10 9 8 7 6 5 4 3 2

Printed and bound in the United States

*for Ellen Rudin*
*who gave Kate the courage to write this book*
*and*
*who made me kiss the mailman*

# Contents

# 1

# Before it began

I met Susannah first.

That's not true really. I did know one of the others before. And I'd heard of the rest, except for Sol. But they weren't real to me. Susannah was, almost from the first moment.

I have a good imagination, of course. Now that I've decided to go back over it all and try to figure out what really went on, maybe I'll start adjusting the facts here and there. I could blame the mistakes on other people and cast myself as the perfect heroine. That way, thinking back wouldn't hurt.

But it wouldn't help either. I think I've been moving toward a new place. It's as though I've been traveling along a freeway where all I could do was go ahead. Now it's ending and there are turn-off signs. If I'm to pick the right road for me, I need first to know the truth about this past year—what place I came from and exactly where I've already been. I feel changed. I want to know why and how.

It shouldn't be that hard. My memory's as good as my imagination and Emily has told me, countless times, that honesty is one of my besetting sins.

What'll I start with though? Some of it happened before I was even born. Oh, I can't begin away back there and keep things in order.

I still say I met Susannah first.

When Emily and I left school together, though, late that afternoon, I had no idea Susannah even existed. The day had been extra bright and shining, the way some days in April are. At noon the sky had been so polished with wind it almost burned you to look at it. Yet you couldn't help looking, and looking again, and then once more and once more. Our school building is big, but that day every time I glanced out the window the classroom walls seemed to squeeze in. I wanted to leap up on my desk and burst into song! I can't stay on key but that seemed utterly irrelevant.

I happen not to mind school. I certainly don't go around making speeches about how great it is, but lots of the time, in spite of myself, I enjoy it. Not French or geography, except once in a long while. The rest of it, though, isn't as dire as they claim. Even so, that afternoon somebody should have come around and pasted up huge official signs on all school doors.

NO KIDS

ALLOWED IN

WHILE

SPRING

LASTS

(I start to think—and already I'm off the track. I guess that's one way I'm like Mother. "Watch that tangent, April," my father warns her. "You'll forget where you left off."

She does forget too. She argues, though, that some of the best conversations take place off on tangents. She should know!)

The brilliance of the day was softening, blurring a little, as Emily and I finally made our escape from "The Brain Box." It was not quite dusk but you could sense the shadows coming. I no longer yearned to explode into freedom. I felt lapped in peace, dreamy, drowsy.

I should have gone on home and started my homework. There was always a project due or a test coming. It even crossed my mind that it would be extremely nice of me to get a real dinner ready for my parents. So often when they come home from the store, we settle for munching on things we can eat out of our hands: bread, chunks of cheese, tomatoes, pickles, fruit. If I hurried, I'd have time to cook meat and potatoes. Instant potatoes, but still, hot.

"I think I'll go home and cook something," I told Emily.

I tried to sound as though I could hardly wait to get to the stove. Emily did not quite let herself smile.

"Okay," she said.

We reached the corner where I'd have to turn. Emily, on her way to baby-sit her cousins, the four Sutherland kids, paused.

"Oh, keep going," I growled and stepped off the curb with her.

Emily did not pretend to be surprised. The Sutherland children are on the diabolical side but I love them. Next to Emily's baby sister Louisa, they used to be my favorite children. (Now they come next to Louisa and Susannah.)

Also I was not in my cooking mood.

I wonder about that. What if I had gone home? Would everything have turned out differently? Perhaps I'd never have found Susannah!

I don't really believe this. Even if nothing else had been the same, she and I would have met somewhere. We were meant to love each other.

I had no premonition though that something important was about to happen. I was thinking back to school.

"Hey, you never showed me your character sketch," I said to Emily.

"Kate Bloomfield, I wish you would slow down!" Emily gasped. "I'm not a giraffe even if you are."

This happens to us all the time. I walk fast and I do have longer legs. We've measured. So I laughed and slowed to a saunter. My saunter is Emily's fast walk.

It was a full minute before it dawned on me that this time something was fishy. Emily was avoiding looking at me. It's queer how you can tell. At least with Emily I can. I was supposed to think she only happened to be gazing at the houses on the other side of the street. Her ears were too pink, though, and her neck too stiff.

Something was on her conscience.

I puzzled over it, guessing there must be a clue in what we'd been saying. We'd talked about me going home. No, that should have been on *my* conscience, not Emily's.

I'd asked about the character sketches. We'd written them the day before during English class and Mr. Armstrong had given them back that afternoon. They had to be about somebody we knew. I'd done mine on Mother and I'd told Emily about it last night.

"Isn't this an absolutely glorious day?" Emily burst out in the phoniest voice I'd heard in my whole life. I knew then. I stopped stock-still.

"Hand it over," I told her.

"I don't have the faintest idea what you're talking about," protested Emily.

It didn't work, of course. Emily Ann Blair is no match for me and she knows it. I'm bigger, to start with, and I get madder, to go on with. Besides, Emily being Emily, most of her wanted to give in and show it to me. She'd probably been waiting for me to ask. I know how it is. I would have wanted to show her too.

She had me down on a page and a half. We moved on slowly as I began to read. She babbled away, telling me she knew it was terrible. I paid no attention. Emily always does that with things she writes—especially when she herself really likes them.

## My Friend Kate

My friend Kate Bloomfield has character. Lots of kids haven't yet, but Kate is different. When she is angry she bangs or turns cold and cutting. I have seen her grow an inch taller through sheer rage. This is not her most endearing quality but it does make knowing her exciting.

She likes to think she's tough. She swaggers and brags. When she is with little children, though, she is gentle and kind. They run to her when they see her coming.

Kate loves words. She writes poems. They hardly ever rhyme and they do not sound poetic but you feel what she means, inside yourself, when she gives you one to read. Her parents own a bookstore. They like words as much as she does.

Kate is a friend who understands what you mean without your always having to say it.

She likes sunsets. She likes animals. She is crazy enough to like math. She hates parsnips, coconut and French.

She is my best friend. Even though she is often a trial to me, I have never met anyone I like better. I believe we will still be friends when we are old, old ladies in wheelchairs.

I read over the last paragraph, stalling for time. Emily was quiet now, waiting. She looked scared.

And she *should* be scared! Telling Mr. Armstrong that I hated parsnips, for crying out loud!

". . . I have never met anyone I like better . . ."

I hadn't either, but it wasn't something a person could come right out and say on the way home from school. Not this person anyway!

"You've finished," Emily said. "Give it back."

I looked at it once more. He'd given her 15 out of 20. He prides himself on being a hard marker.

"I would have given you 16," I said gruffly, passing the sheets of paper over. "But not another mark! Not after that about parsnips!"

Emily laughed outright. She knew I liked it. I didn't have to explain. That's the kind of friends we were.

"You didn't say I was Jewish," I remembered suddenly, thinking back.

Emily thought back too. I could see her checking her own words inside her head and realizing that I was right.

"I guess not," she agreed.

"Why didn't you?"

I wasn't worried about what she'd say. I knew my being Jewish didn't bother Emily any more than her being a Presbyterian troubled me. When we had first begun to make friends, a year and a half before, I hadn't been so sure. It took me months to get around to telling her my Dad was a Jew.

It wasn't that I thought she'd do anything drastic when she found out. I was just scared she'd start treating me as though I were somehow different. (I felt plenty different enough already with both my parents working till all hours, and being the kind of people they are. At that age, every kid wants square parents. Mine are parabolas one minute and ellipses the next.)

But that was ancient history now. I had told

her and nothing important changed between us. It was hard to believe, that afternoon, that there had been a time when the two of us had not been friends. It was impossible to imagine our friendship ending.

So, standing there asking her, I wasn't worried; I was just curious. And Emily, puzzling over her answer, was not embarrassed; she was simply puzzled.

"I was describing your character," she said finally. "You aren't very Jewish, not so it's part of your character. Though really, I guess I just forgot."

I should have been pleased. Maybe I was, a little. Emily thought of me as me, Kate—not as her Jewish friend. But I hadn't needed a character sketch to tell me that. I didn't think of Emily as a gentile either. Once Dad had said to me, "Emily is Emily—and don't you forget it." It had been so obvious I hadn't had any trouble remembering.

Emily thought the subject was closed. She had halted and was putting the loose pages back into her notebook where they belonged. Emily enjoys being tidy. That is one of the things about her that mystify me.

"Didn't my being Jewish even cross your mind?" I persisted. My words surprised both of us.

Emily looked at me.

"If it had, I'd have put it in, wouldn't I?" she said. "Why?"

"Oh, I don't know," I muttered.

She was right, wasn't she? I was not very

Jewish. Hardly Jewish at all. Dad didn't go to the synagogue or not eat pork or do any of the things that I thought went with being a Jew. He had told me that he was proud to be Jewish but he had never told me why. I had meant, for a long time, to talk more to him about it but that wasn't easy. Mother was with us usually. It seemed rude to ask about it with her there. He wasn't home that much either and he was mostly tired and he did like to read.

We all three like to read, for that matter. Lots of evenings we're in the same room, each of us with a different book, and the only thing anyone says is "Listen to this."

The other two always do listen—with half an ear and taking care not to lose their own places. I've picked up a lot of fascinating odds and ends that way. But I had not learned what made my father proud to be a Jew.

Mother isn't proud of being anything. I know because I asked her once.

"Mother, what *are* you exactly?" I stumbled.

It came out of whatever we'd been talking about, so she knew what I was after, but at first she just goofed off. She claimed she was a frustrated beachcomber and a dedicated eavesdropper. I didn't laugh though.

"I'm serious," I protested, sticking with it. "What are you really?"

She propped her elbows on the table and

clutched her head between her hands in a despairing way.

"Oh, Kate, why must I *be* anything?" she groaned. "This business of religion! I believe in the fatherhood of God and the brotherhood of man—I think. Isn't that good enough?"

I didn't think so. When they give you a form to fill in and it says *religion*, they don't leave room in the little box for you to write in "the fatherhood of God and the brotherhood of man."

"Well, would you say you're a . . . a Protestant?"

I meant to ask her if she were a Christian but I lost my nerve in the middle. After all, her parents had been Anglicans, even if they did let it slide. And, once in a blue moon, Mother herself took off and went to church. She didn't explain; she just went. She'd taken me along a few times. I hadn't enjoyed it, but maybe that was because I had to concentrate so hard on doing the right thing at the right moment.

Anyway, asking her if she were a Christian sounded fresh. The trouble was, asking her if she were a Protestant sounded crazy. I waited for her to stare at me. She snapped instead.

"I'd say I'm an Independent," my mother said.

The sharpness in her words slammed the conversation shut. I left it.

I was mad though. Emily and her mother, I knew, would have spent ages discussing the whole thing. Mrs. Blair was forever helping Emily to understand things. Parents, I thought, were supposed to be like that—setting good examples, telling you about right and wrong, teaching and guiding. They were intended to make life plainer, not more complicated.

I did not try pointing this out to Mother. For one thing, her temper has a short fuse. For another, what was the use? I'd watched my older sister Marilyn spend years trying to change Mother. She had not accomplished one thing.

You'd think Marilyn would play some part in all this but she never has had a lot to do with my life. She's so much older and we're different. Marilyn's ladylike. Not only that, she's left home. She lives in Calgary now, with her husband and her little boy. That's a long way away.

One thing I do know though. David, Marilyn's husband, is a Presbyterian. No shilly-shallying around with "the fatherhood of God" for David. And Marilyn's one too, since she married him. (We're quite a family for intermarrying. )

We missed Marilyn when she left home but things were more relaxed too. My big sister always knows the right thing to do and she never loses her temper. Also she does not enjoy reading.

Often she writes how much she likes Calgary.

"She likes it because it makes absolutely no demands on her intellect," Mother commented one day.

"Geography has nothing to do with intellect, April," Dad told her. "You aren't being fair."

Mother raised her eyebrows at him.

"Being fair isn't one of my great, shining goals in life," she said.

I tried to figure out whether they were insulting Marilyn or Calgary and who was doing what. Mother must have noticed because she did an about-face.

"Really, of course, I'm delighted Marilyn's happy," she announced for my benefit.

"And just what is your definition of happiness?" Dad challenged.

They were off then, stealing each other's arguments, attacking, defending, then attacking their own side. In no time, they'd lost sight of Marilyn completely and were having a marvelous time in their world of words. When I go back over some of my parents' conversations I have less trouble understanding my own confusion about practically everything. With them, nothing is clear; nothing is final; nothing is easy. And everything has three sides.

"Hi, you two," Emily said, breaking in on my jumble of thoughts.

We had arrived at the Sutherlands'. Two little girls were out in front of the house. One was Jean Sutherland; the other I had never seen before. I smiled at Jean.

It is hard to believe, but in that first moment I didn't notice Susannah at all.

# 2

# I meet Susannah

The two children did not notice us either until Emily spoke. They had tied one of those long plastic skipping ropes to the porch railing and they were trying to skip. They stopped while Jean came speeding over to hug first Emily and then me. Jean is the huggingest child I know. I think it comes from being in the middle of all the others. She wants to make certain you notice she's there.

"Mother saw you and Kate coming so she went ahead and left because she had to take a casserole and she was going to be late," Jean explained, all in one breath. "The boys and Ann are inside watching TV," she added.

She made the entire speech with an air of

great importance as though she were Private
Secretary to the Queen. I grinned but Emily listened gravely.

"Thank you, Jeanie," she said at the end.
"You're a fine messenger."

Jean gave a small bounce of delight and then,
looked modestly at her toes. I was sorry I'd
almost laughed at her, as I started to follow
Emily up the walk to the house.

"Oh, Em-i-lee, can't Kate stay out with us?"
Jean begged.

She was using her baby voice. It's a cross
between a lisp and a whine. I know she just does
it to get attention but I stopped feeling sorry I'd
smiled.

"Oh, puh-leeze, Em-leee!" It sounded as though
she were pleading for her life to be spared.

The family policy is "Ignore the whine and
it'll go away." The only trouble is, you can see
them doing the ignoring. Their lips tighten and
their voices get clipped and terribly brisk. Jean
likes making them do exactly that, I'm certain. It
works with me every time. I struggled not to but
I could feel myself stiffening. She can't win with
Emily though. When it comes to handling those
Sutherlands, Emily is some kind of super being
with added powers.

"Kate can do whatever she pleases," she said
easily, smiling at me over her shoulder. "I'll be
getting supper. I *know* how you long to help get
supper, Katharine."

"I'll stay out," I answered.

Baby voice or no baby voice, Jean was one of my favorite people, and usually I would have chosen to stay outside just because she'd asked me. That night, though, it wasn't so simple. Emily must have guessed as much.

"Don't you two pester her," she told the kids. "She's had a hard day."

She made me sound like an overworked businessman but I didn't care. I didn't feel like going in and getting caught in the whirlwind of activity that is Ann and the two boys. I had no wish to jump rope either. Jean had not introduced her friend and I wasn't even curious about her, although it did occur to me that she must be new in town. Might be, anyway. Riverside is no village. She could have been around there all her life and I'd just not encountered her before.

Emily disappeared. I sat down on the steps. Jean stood, for an instant, studying my face. I knew she was there but my thoughts were crowding back in on me. I guess I sort of looked right through her. She sighed. Then, without another word to me, the two small girls returned to their skipping.

With the small part of my mind that had registered Jean's sigh, I realized that I had not yet heard the other child speak. She was clearly older than Jean although she wasn't much bigger. She reminded me, vaguely, of a graceful twig. She had on a very short pleated skirt and it blew up around her each time she jumped.

Jean chanted for both of them.

*Down in the valley*
*Where the green grass grows . . .*

I went back to trying to decide why it bothered me that Emily did not think my being Jewish was important. I couldn't keep my mind on it.

*Down in the valley*
*Where the—*

The chant broke off and began again. Over and over and over!

*Down in the—*

*Down in the valley*
*Where the green—*

*Down in the val—*

*Down in the valley*
*Where—*

*Down—*

I had to look. They were taking turns trying to run in and they were fouling it up every time.

Jean was really too young. Her feet weren't coordinated. The other one would have been able to do it, I thought; she moved as lightly as a bird. When Jean turned for her, though, the rope slapped around and sort of half-dragged, not keeping the rhythm. So she tripped too.

I knew I should get up and go to their rescue. The Kate Bloomfield that Emily had written about would have.

But I wasn't feeling like that Kate Bloomfield. It was the character sketch itself that was pulling at my attention. I was wondering whether I did, in fact, swagger. (I've decided I do.) And I was shying away from, and at the same moment clutching close, what Emily had said about my poems. I wished I could remember her exact words. Of course, I could always get her to let me read the thing again. Or could I? What would I say to her?

"Emily . . . um . . . by the way . . ." I began, under my breath, practicing sounding casual, and not succeeding.

"Down in the valley—" puffed a small stubborn voice. Then, despairing, it wailed, "Oh, I WISH we could do it!"

It was as though I were suddenly a marionette. Jean's words twitched at me. Much as I wanted to stay where I was, they were pulling me to my feet. In one second they would have marched me over to that skipping rope.

"Jeanie," called Emily, "your sandwich is ready."

Jean dropped the rope and ran. I settled back, guilty because I was so glad. Now the other child would take off and I would have myself to myself.

The whole long dazzle of that April afternoon shone again within me, in that one instant. If I could catch it in words . . .

I might have turned it into a poem but I didn't because right then I saw that the small girl I did not know was still there. And I didn't have to write a poem; I was watching one.

I sat without stirring, like a rock, like a tree, like a curve of sky. Yet, if I had moved, she would not have noticed. She had gone deep into a private world. There she stood and turned the skipping rope smoothly, beautifully. As it twirled, not missing a beat, she recited for somebody only she could see. This time, the words sang through without a break, without even a pause.

> *Down in the valley*
> *Where the green grass grows,*
> *There sat Susannah*
> *Pretty as a rose.*
> *She sang and she sang*
> *And she sang so sweet*
> *Along came a boy and*
> *Kissed her on the cheek.*

When she reached the end, she went back to the beginning. Softly, softly, she sang through the chant again.

Dusk blurs the world into a dream place, puts everything under a spell. The child was part of that magic. Yet she was not unreal. For me, suddenly, she was the one real thing. Somehow she made being, plain old everyday being, something newly discovered, something to take time over and feel good about.

"What's your name?" I asked.

My stupid too-loud words ran over her small song and flattened it. I was appalled. I sounded exactly like a mother trying to make friends.

The girl did not draw back from me and my question, though, the way I think I would have done. (The way I often still do. )

She let the rope drop. Her bright short pleats, which had blown so gaily, now hung down in a neat orange circle, very well behaved. She stopped swaying. Although she stood facing me and even seemed to be looking right at me, I knew the music of the jump-rope rhyme still held her back so that she was, for a moment, caught between worlds.

Then she shrugged it away and spoke.

"Would you call me Susannah?" she asked.

She was so serious. She kept her head up but I knew she was shy. She was braced, ready for me to laugh at her. Yet, if I did, she would be hurt.

"Sure," I told her quickly.

My voice no longer sounded phony. I did smile but only just. She knew I wasn't laughing at her. She smiled back widely.

"I'm named Susan actually," she confided.

Still holding onto the rope, she came nearer. Her eyes were enormous the instant she was serious; when she smiled, they narrowed until they almost disappeared.

"But I'd like to try being called Susannah. We have an old book at home—"

"*Susannah of the Mounties?*" I guessed.

"Yes," she cried, her eyes widening again in astonishment and admiration at my ability to read minds. I was just lucky. That Susannah was the only book-Susannah I knew.

"That's not my favorite," she put in hastily. "Have you read the one where she goes to boarding school in England?"

I nodded and agreed that I too liked it better. We knew something important about each other right then, Susannah and I—we shared a friend.

Five minutes later, we had retied the skipping rope in the middle so we had two ends free to turn and I was teaching her Double Dutch. I was absolutely right about her ability to skip. She was fantastic. Just watching her bob up and down, her long dark braids flying, made me feel old and infirm.

Then the others came trooping out, all of them this time, and we switched to Hide-and-Seek because everybody could do that. I was It.

I caught Ann first, of course. She gets so excited she can't stay still. She also squeaks when you come near her. The rest weren't so easy. I'd never have got the boys. They had crawled in under the verandah where it's all dirt and spiders. As a rule, I wouldn't let spiders and dirt stand in my way but I still had on my school clothes. James decided they should ambush me, though, and they leaped out as I went by. I screamed the way they hoped I would, but I also ran for Home and caught them both out. Long legs are a decided asset when you are playing Hide-and-Seek.

Then Ann was It.

The minute I saw her squeeze her eyes tight shut and begin to concentrate on counting, I knew where I'd hide. School clothes and all, I went right up the tree she was leaning against and perched in the branches over her head. It is a sturdy pine with wide, welcoming branches, so it didn't sway; but anyone but Ann would have heard me climbing. Ann, though, has such a time when she counts. She can only get to ten dependably. So she goes that far, turns down a finger and starts at one again. When she had completed both hands, she called out

> *One hundred!*
> *Ready or not*
> *You must be caught*
> *Hiding around the goal*
> *Or not.*
> *O-U-T spells OUT*

*And out you must go!*
*Here I come!*

I was hiding around the goal all right. I looked right down on the top of her head. I wasn't even hiding. All she had to do was look up.

She didn't. She began to hunt. My eyes searched with her and, in less than a minute, I'd found everybody. Emily was lying flat in the canvas hammock. Jean was under the steps. ( I couldn't see her but I'd watched her when she hid.) James was behind the barberry bush. John was up in the Manitoba Maple on the other side of the yard. (Copycat!) Susannah was flattened into the corner where the verandah joins the house.

Ann wandered around the yard. She looked small and without hope. Watching her, I remembered how it felt to be It when everyone else was bigger and quicker and smarter. I decided to give her one more minute and then cough.

Susannah beat me to it. I saw her edge out a bit so that she was half in the open.

Ann didn't notice.

Susannah swung one arm back and forth.

Ann still didn't see.

Susannah eased out a step further. She didn't come all the way. I knew why. She didn't want Ann to guess that she was doing it on purpose.

I thought, Ann, look. Open your eyes and *look*!

As if she had caught my unspoken signal, the smaller girl stiffened.

"I see you, Susan!" she yelled, and then headed for my tree.

Susan ran after her, but slowly. When Ann stumbled and went down on one knee, I knew I was right about what Susannah was up to. She waited for Ann to scramble to her feet before she began to jog after her again.

"One, two, three on Susan!" Ann shouted, touching base.

"Hey, Ann," Susan said, her soft voice carrying clearly up to me, "have you really looked close to home?"

Ann stared around helplessly, seeing only the empty yard. I knew I was caught, though, and I was right again. My new friend pointed. Ann peered up and screamed joyfully, "One, two, three on Kate! Now, I've got two!"

She was taking the entire credit. Neither of us minded a bit. She ran off to look for the others. She no longer looked little and lonely. Susannah and I swapped smiles.

My friend noticed, at that instant, how late it was. The lawn was all shadow now.

"I have to go," she gasped. "Bye!"

She sped away down the darkening street, turning just once to wave. The next minute, Emily emerged from the hammock and started rounding up the Sutherlands for baths. The game was over.

I lingered by my friendly tree. I was filled with a strange excitement. I heard the kids complaining about having to go inside but I didn't really listen. Instead I stared off down the street where Susannah had vanished.

I love that dopey little kid, I thought. She's like Emily. No, she's not. But she's my friend, like Emily.

I laughed at myself then. Kids my age don't have eight-year-olds for friends. They're okay and everything but this Susan was Jean's friend, not mine.

I followed the others into the house.

Then, as I moved to close the door, shutting out the twilight, I saw the skipping rope left lying on the walk. Susannah had been so beautiful standing in the late afternoon light, singing and turning the rope for herself.

"That Susannah!" I said to Emily helplessly.

"I thought her name was Susan," Emily said. "James, go on up those stairs this instant!"

"Susan what?" I asked.

Nobody was listening. Even if somebody had been, none of them knew her last name. None of them knew her private inside name either. To all of them, she was just Susan.

"Sometimes she's kooky," Jean observed, out of the blue. "Susan is a nuthead," Ann singsonged.

I turned on her sharply. Didn't she understand what Susan had done for her a few minutes before? But she didn't, of course, and what's more, Susan hadn't meant her to. I kept quiet.

The two Sutherland girls ran toward the

stairs, as Emily had ordered. My hand, raised perhaps to shake Ann—I'm not sure—dropped. I felt silly.

Yet, for one startling instant, I had been swept by a gust of deep anger. I knew then. I didn't understand why, but Susannah—skinny, dreamy, bookish Susannah with her pretending and her kind heart—was going to matter to me. I couldn't shut her out. Even if I wanted to, it was too late. She mattered already.

# 3

# Me at home

It was dark when I went home.

Mother and Dad were still sitting at the table. They had had their first cup of coffee. I could tell because Dad smiled at me right away. Not that he doesn't smile at me often. He does, but neither of them is given to smiling for at least an hour after they come home from work. Running a paperback bookstore takes a lot of smiling. Also, although there are chairs in the store, the two of them stand up all day. I don't expect them to be friendly until they've been sitting down and have snapped and snarled a bit and have eaten something and had coffee. Then they are restored and it is safe to treat them like people.

"Hi," I said, glad I hadn't come home sooner.

"Good evening, Katharine," my father said.

My name really is Katharine but he's the only one who calls me by it. Oh, the others do when they are mad or kidding but he does it all the time. I'd mind if it were anybody else, but from him, it's okay. If he stopped calling me Katharine, I'd feel an important piece of me were lost.

Mother did not speak. It was a moment before I noticed her deafening silence. Then I checked. I'd guessed right. She was giving me one of her Looks. When she does it, she arches her eyebrows nearly out of sight and her nose seems to get longer. Her mouth stitches into a thin line. It is supposed to make me feel guilty, but it doesn't work too well. I usually only feel especially fond of her. She's trying so hard to behave like a mother but she always misses it somehow.

I wasn't sure what I'd done this time but I looked downcast. (I think I missed looking downcast somehow too.)

"One of these days, young woman, I'm going to come in and find you not here and *worry!*" my mother announced.

I thought that was unlikely but it was nice of her to say so. She does wonder sometimes, I know, but not worry. Talking to other mothers gets her stirred up, every so often, and she feels obliged to panic. Still, underneath, she knows I'm no delinquent. I talk a lot tougher than I act.

Also, we've gone our separate ways since I

was a baby and she hired somebody to look after me and went to work with Dad. We're both used to being independent and she likes it as much as I do.

She does love me though. And I love her. In our own ways. It is not the way Emily and her mother love each other but I wouldn't switch. I used to think I would, when I was younger, but now, though I like Mrs. Blair, I wouldn't want to belong to her. She wants to know too much about what's going on inside you. Emily doesn't mind sharing. I would.

I love Dad too. Maybe I love him more. I really don't know whether that's true or not. Mothers do bother at you but there is something trustworthy about them. Even their bad moods are predictable.

Right then, I was finding Dad hard to figure out. I was used to his smile kind of lingering, for instance, and when Mother began taking me apart, he'd be right in there saving me, making her laugh, calming her down. That night, his smile was over almost before I'd seen it. Already he not only was not rushing to my rescue, he'd stopped listening.

At that time, I still had not fully taken in the fact that my parents had private lives of their own which had nothing to do with me. I believed, part of the time anyway, that I was the center of their universe. When they got preoccupied, I wondered what I'd done.

I must say they had never encouraged this notion of mine. Anything but! Still, I guess it's natural enough wanting to be important to the people you love. And I am important to them. It's just that I'm not the sole star in their sky.

My father had discovered who had moved to town recently, that was all. His grouchiness had not one thing to do with me. I did not know this then. But neither could I think of anything I'd done to upset him.

Meanwhile, Mother was still waiting. She was tapping her foot by now.

"I already ate," I said, hoping to distract her.

"Slim, did you hear that?" My mother addressed my father as though he were a meeting. She gave a magnificent flourish with one hand, underlining her next words.

"She informs us she has eaten. Not where, mind you! Not with whom! She—has—eaten!"

"Oh, April, leave her be," Dad said.

He usually enjoys her carrying on like that. Both she and I were startled.

"Now *what* has come over *you*?" Mother said.

My mother does not dodge issues, not unimportant ones anyway. Neither is she the soul of tact.

Dad was not telling, however.

"Nothing has come over me. I would like another cup of coffee if anyone around here has the strength to get it," he snapped.

Mother snapped right back. She always does—and then, too late, she's sorry.

"The jar's right where it always is," she said. "Kate and I have worked as hard as you have all day long."

Dad glowered. I reached quickly for his cup and got there before he did. Mother opened her mouth, thought better of it, and left well enough alone. There was a silence between them while I waited for the kettle to boil. I had my back to them. I didn't want to turn around but at last I did.

"Well, what exciting thing happened in school today?" Mother asked brightly.

I was mad. She wasn't even looking at me, for crying out loud!

"The building burned down. The principal ran off with his secretary. Seventy kids were caught smoking marijuana in the schoolyard at noon. Anything else you'd like to know?" I said.

Mother sucked in a deep breath, smacked both hands down flat on the table, started to tower to her full five feet four—and fell back, laughing.

"Oh Kate, I'm sorry," she gasped. "Honestly I am. Tell us . . . *did* something exciting happen? This time, I promise, I'm listening."

Mother isn't hard to forgive sometimes.

Mentally I ran back over the day. It had been long and full and different but I didn't know what to say about it to them.

There was no point in beginning "The sun was shining!" BLOOMFIELDS' BOOKS has an enormous bow window and, also, whenever it is the least bit warm outside, Mother stands the door ajar. The smell of coffee, the sight of chairs, and the books themselves act like magnets on tired shoppers. My parents would not only know about the good weather; they were probably sick to death of hearing about it.

I thought about school, but we hadn't started to study a new play or anything. That's the only kind of school talk that really interests those two.

"There must have been something," Mother urged.

She had made up her mind to be a Good Listener now and she was counting on me to provide her with some material. Every inch of her was a Mother Devoting Her Undivided Attention to Her Child. I caught my father smiling again, just a little. Well, she *is* funny. I was careful not to look at him again. Mother was taking herself seriously. There was no need for us to hurt her.

I could tell them about Susannah, I thought.

How could I, though, really? What was there to say?

Emily's character sketch?

No. I mean, how would I? It seemed terribly private, all at once.

"Sheila was her usual obnoxious self," I said, clutching at straws and coming up with the one person in all the world I thoroughly disliked. Then, before they got curious about Sheila, I was inspired. I knew exactly what Mother would like to hear.

"Lindsay gave John Hollingsforth back that bracelet of his. Her mother made her," I announced.

"Who's Sheila?" Dad asked as I spoke.

What would have happened if I had told him about her then? Would he have said anything? Would things have worked out differently?

I'll never know. It is surprising that his words even registered in my mind. Mother was already off on a tirade about Lindsay Ross, as I had known she would be.

Mothers are outright ridiculous every so often.

Lindsay Ross, Emily Blair, and I had been friends—like people called us the Three Musketeers and that kind of thing (James Sutherland said The Three Stooges)—until the past Christmas holidays. Oh, we were still friends. Whenever she saw us in passing, Lin waved and smiled. She still called me on the phone. But at Christmas, she and John Hollingsforth had discovered each other, and by March they were going steady and Lin hadn't much time to spare.

Here is a shining example of the idiocy of mothers. Finally, the Saturday before, John had given Lin his identification bracelet. We all knew they were going together, but as of then it became official. And from the fuss, you'd think they were Romeo and Juliet about to elope! My mother, who never did like Lindsay much anyway, stormed; Emily's mother screamed blue murder; Lin's own mother . . . well, it passes description. She even managed to get Lin's father hot and bothered, which he is usually far from. So good old Lindsay, who can't be bothered fighting but who always gets her own way in the end, simply and sweetly told her mother she'd give the bracelet back. All the adults sighed with relief and simmered down. Disaster had been averted! What they didn't know was she just traded the bracelet for a ring of his, a silly plastic one he got out of one of those junky machines—like the ones for bubble gum except these cost a dime. I'd seen the ring with my own eyes that morning. Lin had it on a chain around her neck.

"It's even more romantic," she told me when we were changing after gym and Emily and I got a chance to view it.

Needless to say, I did not mention this to Mother. I relaxed and let her rave happily about Lindsay being still just a child and what a good thing she had come to her senses.

I knew though (and I was absolutely right) that nothing had changed between Lin and John. By now, she's had the identification bracelet back for ages. I wouldn't be surprised if they end up marrying each other in ten years or so. Lin will want the right equipment first. She's already collecting silver—and she's *pleased* about it. (Anybody giving me a teaspoon for a present will wait a long time for a thank-you letter!) John *is* good-looking. He's no brain but he's brighter than Lin. She flutters around him. She feels sorry for Emily and me; she says we haven't lived. As Emily says, "If that's life, help!"

(Of course if one David Nelson should discover *me*, I might see things differently. Not that he's about to. He remembers me climbing trees in Grade Five and he doesn't seem to notice that I've given them up. Except when I need one. As in a game of Hide-and-Seek. Thank the stars he didn't happen along and see me. I'd have died. Or invited him to play. He just might have done it too. Dave's wonderful with kids. Lots of them have crushes on him. Little kids and me and Emily and practically every other girl I know. But Dave Nelson is *not* part of this story. Forget him, Katharine.)

What with gossiping about Lindsay and then doing homework, it got to be bedtime. I was almost asleep, as a matter of fact, when I made the mistake of thinking of Sheila again.

Dad had asked me who she was, I realized, and I had not answered. He hadn't asked again so it didn't really matter. I did my best to shoo Sheila out of my mind.

But, in spite of myself, I was waking up.

I tried being sensible. I reminded myself that I couldn't have told him much anyway. Her family had not been in town long, only a month or so. She had an older brother in college somewhere and her father was a doctor. None of that would be of particular interest to Dad. And that was my sum total of information about Sheila.

Except for the fact that you don't like her, a voice inside me put in. Except for the fact that you cannot stand her, to be honest.

But suppose I had told Dad that? I knew exactly what he would say. "Why?" he'd want to know. Reasonably, quietly, sensibly—and he'd expect me to be reasonable too. There was nothing reasonable about my feelings when it came to Sheila.

"Forget her!" I said aloud, thumping my pillow over.

I mean, what was there to think about her anyway? Who cared about her big-shot brother, or her father either? What was it about her that kept bugging me?

I knew. Oh, I knew.

But, even to myself, I wasn't about to give in and say it.

Think about Emily, I told myself.

I did think about her and I smiled in the darkness. "Old ladies in wheelchairs." I pictured us. Emily would be a spry old lady from years of running to keep up to me. I wondered what would force her to take to a wheelchair. Exhaustion maybe.

I relaxed and drifted again toward sleep. At once, uninvited, Sheila came thrusting back into my consciousness.

I fought her off.

Think about . . . think about Susannah, I commanded.

I thought about Susannah. At first, the image

of her also made me smile but, almost immediately, my smile vanished.

I did not know who Susannah was. I might never see her again.

I tried to reason my way around it. I could find out easily enough. I only had to ask. Ask whom? It would be no use to ask the Sutherlands. I already had. They just knew that the girl's name was Susan. They had met her in the park near their place. She had come home from the park with Jean to skip rope.

I wondered how many girls in Riverside were named Susan. Dozens, for sure. Maybe hundreds.

I could not feature myself hanging around a park after school on the off chance of someday spotting one eight-year-old kid. It was a big park, to begin with. We could both be there day after day and still miss each other.

The thing was getting wildly out of proportion. That happens at night. Silly little puzzles blow up into huge problems and you're too tired to keep cool about them. I reminded myself of this fact. I also told myself firmly that Susannah might be nice but she was still only a kid.

So if you don't see her again, so what? I said.

Being sensible. Acting my age.

Then . . . *Would you call me Susannah?* I heard a small voice ask.

Once more I smiled. I could not help it. There she was—long thin legs, short dancing pleats, shining braids and big, shy eyes.

Yet she had not been shy with me. Okay. I'd keep watching for her. I wouldn't go hunting especially; I wasn't right out of my mind. But Riverside wasn't Toronto, for heaven's sake. She'd turn up. She'd be bound to.

*Down in the valley*
*Where the green grass grows,*
*There sat Susannah*
*Pretty as a rose . . .*

The skipping rhyme worked like a lullaby. Forgetting Sheila at last, I slept.

# 4

# My friend and my foe

I stepped out the door into a Scotch mist. That's what Mrs. Blair calls it anyway. It's wetter than a mist really but drier than a drizzle. If you can walk a block or two, feeling its coolness on your face and breathing in long fresh gulps of it, and then go back into your house and dry off and be warm, a Scotch mist is enjoyable. I could not go back in. By the time I reached Emily's front door, I was definitely damp. Morose too.

"I don't believe yesterday ever happened," I grumbled as we started out for school. "To think I actually imagined that spring had arrived!"

"But it has, Kate. It has!" Emily enthused.

She was still feeling the coolness on her face and breathing those long fresh gulps. I turned up my collar and glowered.

"Well, if that was spring, what happened to summer? It comes next. Today isn't spring and it certainly isn't summer. It's like November."

"No, no, Katharine. This *is* spring!"

Emily lifted her face to the dismal heavens with a look of idiotic bliss. The drizzle (it *was* a drizzle now) spattered in her eyes but she was so far gone she didn't even blink.

"This," she informed me, "is an April shower. This is what starts the flowers growing. Oh, Kate, honestly, don't you love it? It's so refreshing!"

The heavens must be immune to flattery. Or maybe they thought Emily wanted more. They opened with a rush, and gallons of water came sluicing down on us.

We were both wearing raincoats but we were bareheaded. I don't own a rainhat. (I doubt if Mother's heard of them. ) And Emily's mother had made such a thing over her putting one on, a few minutes before, that Emily had felt called upon to rebel.

"April shower!" I gasped. "April downpour, you mean!"

Then we ran, ducking our heads to protect our faces. Not that running helped. We were wet through in seconds, raincoats and all.

Over and over, I got ahead of her and had to wait. Each time I stopped and looked back, I couldn't help laughing. Emily was having such a struggle to keep from drowning in her own hair. A mass of it would swing out and slap her in the face; then it would just cling, blinding and choking her, till she raked it away. If I could have taken her books she might have managed better, but I had some extras from the library and, bundling them awkwardly under my coat, I had all I could handle.

"If I only had an elastic!" Emily panted, fighting her way into the open again.

That shows how desperate she was. Emily does not believe in putting elastics on her hair. Not unless they are covered elastics. Ordinary rubber bands would ruin it. My mother says Emily has a Rapunzel fixation.

My short hair was plastered flat against my skull by now and cold little rivers of water were running from it right down my back. Compared with Emily's crowning glory though, it was nothing. Still, for once, school appeared a haven to us both. We were almost late. The rest of the kids had gone into the room, although puddles on the floor showed that others, too, had been caught in the rain.

"Hurry," I told Emily.

I had given my head a quick shake as we came into the building. Already my hair was beginning to revive a little. In less than an hour, it would be dry and shaggy again. Emily looked at herself in the mirror she'd stuck up inside the locker door and she moaned.

I stood and considered my friend. She looked like a dunked spaniel, those terribly sad ones with the extra long limp ears. She had reason to moan. I could see that. When her hair is dry and combed, it is a deep brown, almost as dark as Susannah's, and it is thick and straight and shining. It is almost down to her waist. Not quite— but she's working on it. I have to admit that if I were Emily, I'd have a Rapunzel fixation myself.

"It is a MESS!" Emily wailed. "I'll have to put it in a braid!"

You'd think she was announcing that this was the Day of the Bomb. For some insane reason, Emily loathes wearing her hair in a braid. I have never been able to understand this. I'd keep mine that way the whole time if I had enough hair, hair like Emily's, that is. If I had hair like Sheila's now, I'd . . . well, first, I'd have it cut as short as possible and hope for the best. If that didn't help, I'd look into buying wigs.

My hair may be wiry and kind of wild but it goes with the rest of me. Sheila's is skinny, all different lengths and split ends. Bits of it are nearly as long as Emily's but most of it is just not going to make it. Also it is a depressing color.

Brown? I guess you'd have to call it brown. There is no such thing as dull dark beige hair, is there? So it is brown. But not nut-brown or wheat-brown or taffy or honey or cinnamon. Let's see. It is the color of a baked apple.

I give up. Nobody, but nobody, has baked-apple-brown hair. Nobody but Sheila, that is.

All this time, Emily had been putting on quite a performance with *her* hair. First she leaned forward, let it all sort of slosh together, gathered it in her two hands and wrung it out the way you would a towel. Then she forced a comb through it, wincing as the tangles caught. Next she set about dividing it. She held a third of it between her teeth while she split the rest evenly. A couple of seconds later, she removed that piece (which had looked like a huge comic mustache) from her mouth and started braiding it in. I grinned—at the mustache effect, I think.

"You should see *your* hair!" commented my best friend in a voice like acid.

I let it pass. I knew how I looked and it didn't worry me. I also knew Emily was truly suffering in a funny way. She isn't conceited; she just knows how good she looks. And looking like that takes living up to.

"What'll I hold it together with?" Emily asked, forgetting about being nasty.

I thought fast and reached for my lunch. Emily looked skeptical as I fished out my plastic sandwich bag, untwisted the wire-and-paper fastener, and offered it to her.

"I guess if it works it's better than nothing," she said, really going out of her way to be grateful.

It did work. It looked a bit strange, mind you. As though Emily's long, dark braid were a garbage bag. I did not say that.

"The very latest thing," I comforted her. "Come on!"

Automatically, as we entered the room, I checked for Sheila. Her desk stood empty. What with no sunshine and no Sheila, I was able to concentrate. I don't remember anything specific I learned but I do remember having the feeling that I was being educated.

At about three, the sky cleared bit by bit. Everything gleamed and looked new in the sudden sunlight. I scribbled a note and held my paper where Emily would see.

> You were right, after all.
> It was an April shower.
> Hurray for spring!

Emily grinned and wrote back:

> Three cheers, if you please!
> Don't be so stingy!

Why I remember all that—us getting caught in the rain, Emily and her braid, the day in school, the notes we wrote each other when the sun came out—I have no idea. There's nothing significant about any of it, nothing that leads up to anything that happened later. Maybe it is just because it happened to Emily and me together before things got muddled. I remember the two of us laughing and almost fighting, but not really, and . . . and simply being friends. It was great. And neither of us stopped, for even one moment, to think how great it was. Not then.

It was as though we owned a fortune in diamonds and we wore them for everyday, wore them as thoughtlessly as though we'd got them at Woolworth's. But isn't that how you should wear diamonds maybe? And friendships.

I'm not sure anymore. I only know it was good then. Better than good. And I thought it would last forever.

That same afternoon, I saw Susannah for the second time. She was coming down Marlborough Hill in great bounding leaps. Dad and I were in the car and couldn't stop. I got excited. I hadn't invented her. There she was!

"Did you see that little girl?" I asked.

"The one trying to fly?" my father said.

"That's Susannah," I told him, loving him for seeing her like that.

I went on then. She was easier to explain than I had thought. When Dad listens at all, he really listens. I described her turning the rope and chanting to herself alone.

"Most children are poets," Dad said. "It takes time and effort to kill the imagination."

"Susannah isn't just 'most children' though," I protested.

Dad smiled. "She did look especially winged," he agreed.

Then Sheila came back to school. It had been

a good week for me. Suddenly, I made up my mind I'd make it even better. After all, the kid was new. She probably felt left out. For once, I'd ignore the way she made my hackles rise. (That's another of Mrs. Blair's expressions.) I'd be friendly.

We were both at our desks before the bell rang.

"Sheila," I plunged in, "I'll help you with the math you missed if you want."

I meant to sound gracious. Maybe it didn't come out that way. I'm not given to graciousness.

"Thanks a lot, Kate," Sheila said, her voice piercing and nasty as a needle, "but when I need your help, I'll ask for it."

My face went red. Purple even. I felt as though she'd spat at me in front of about five hundred people. I did not say one word back. I couldn't. There were no words anywhere. The bell rang. We rose for "O Canada!" I was exceptionally busy all morning. I didn't look at Sheila again. I didn't look at Emily either. She would have looked sorry and I couldn't have stood it.

On the way home, though, I had come around. I was furious. I grilled Emily.

"How did I look when she—you know—" I asked.

"Proud," Emily tried to console me. "Haughty."

I longed to believe her but I was pretty sure I'd looked more stunned than anything. I pictured myself, eyes popping, mouth ajar. I got madder. Suddenly, finally, it was all too much for me.

"I positively loathe that girl," I exploded. "I mean, what did I *do*? I was ready to be friends. You saw that, Emily, didn't you? I was just being friendly."

"Sure you were," Emily said.

She did not put much conviction into it.

"But she's insulted before you even speak to her," I raged on. "Ever since she came, she's looked down her nose at everybody. Well, everybody in *our* class anyway! She likes Jackie Bernstein!"

"She seems to," Emily agreed. "Now let's forget her. Who cares what she thinks? Let's plan what we'll do Saturday."

Changing the subject was a smart move but I was having no part of it.

"What I don't understand is, what's eating her?" I faced Emily now, forcing her to stand still. "I mean, I really want to know. I think she's paranoid."

"Oh, Kate," snorted my friend. "Quit showing off your big vocabulary. You don't even know what that means."

"Okay, so she's not paranoid," I admitted, backing up half an inch. "But just tell me this. Who does she think she is?"

Emily gave me one of her patient looks. They remind me of my father. Or, maybe, her mother. Then she sighed and gave in. I guess she figured if that was what I wanted, she might as well get it over with.

"Sheila's Jewish, for one thing," said Emily.

# 5

# Practically a fight

"So am I!" I said finally.

At last it had been said. I'd badgered Emily into getting it out in the open. Now let her talk her way out of it.

I wasn't admitting, yet, that I wanted her to talk *my* way out of it too.

What did being Jewish have to do with how Sheila Rosenthal was acting? What did being Jewish have to do with anything, for that matter?

"She's *really* Jewish though, Kate," Emily tried again.

"SO AM I!"

I was so angry I was shouting. I'd show her. I'd show Emily and Sheila both.

"Kate Bloomfield, you shut up and let me finish!" Emily yelled.

I was thunderstruck. Emily yelling! I gaped at her.

"Honestly," she went on in her ordinary voice, except more exasperated, "you have some nerve, picking on Sheila Rosenthal. You are every bit as bad. Maybe worse! I'm still not finished!" she snapped as I drew breath.

We were both quiet while a couple of boys pushed past us. When they were gone, I still said nothing. Let her speak her piece. She took her time, using the silence to collect her thoughts. Emily doesn't dash into an argument.

"Now listen," she started.

I already was listening so I refrained from comment. I saw her flush. She didn't want to go on with this, but I knew Emily. Once she was this far, even if I had forced her to begin, she would not back out. That is one of the things which had made us friends. We could talk with each other about things which weren't easy to talk about. This was going to be one of those things. I knew it and so did Emily.

"I am listening," I said.

The words were seconds late and they came out stiffly, but they were a peace offering. Emily caught that. She looked relieved. She also gave up beating about the bush.

"If you'd listened in the first place, you would have heard me say 'for one thing.'" She started back at the beginning. "There are probably lots of other things. She's a stranger. That's one. But her being Jewish might have something to do with it too. We don't know one thing about what her life was like before she came here. Maybe somebody picked on her, hurt her even, and she's waiting for it to happen again. Just in case, she attacks first. I'll grant you, she doesn't delay her attack for long!"

Emily grinned. I knew she was replaying that skirmish in class. It still wasn't funny to me. I went on listening.

"Or, for all we know, Kate, she may have dumb parents who have deliberately taught her the world is out to get her. Her mother might be like Dave Nelson's." She looked at me sideways.

I nodded. I wasn't agreeing exactly. I was just admitting that I knew what she meant about Mrs. Nelson. She is one weird woman. She's part native and she's an atheist. What makes her weird, though, isn't either of those things. It's the way she goes around telling people and telling people that she's part native and an atheist. Then she waits and watches for them to hesitate or blush or anything. Whatever they do, it shows they are against atheists and natives. So she writes another letter to the paper about bigotry in Riverside. Dave and his father are marvelous. They're both fantastically loyal. They never say a word against her But they manage to be friends with all the "bigots" in town.

Emily had a point. If your mother was a Mrs. Nelson and you believed every word she told you, you'd be convinced everyone was against you. You might even be right. Mrs. Nelson hasn't any friends that I know of. She's scared people off, watching them so hard.

"Well, suppose that is how it is, it wouldn't be Sheila's fault she's . . . paranoid, would it?" Emily challenged, falling back on my word for want of a better one.

"She's no baby," I argued. "She ought to be ready to give people a chance before she decides about them. Dave's not like his mother."

I did not look at Emily. I didn't need to.

"Forget Dave. He's lived here all his life, and you know perfectly well his father cancels her out," Emily cleared up my confusion crisply. "Sheila is a stranger, remember! And she probably does feel different. After all, she's the only one in our class who's—"

She caught herself in time and rushed on, not allowing me to break in.

"Okay, Kate, okay! I *know* you are Jewish. You've told me often enough. But it just isn't the same. The Rosenthals send Sheila to the rabbi for lessons in Hebrew. History, too, I think Jackie said Jewish kids study, when she made that speech."

"Emily, if you'd—" I managed to insert.

Emily shot one hand toward me as though to clap it over my mouth. She thought she knew what I was thinking. She was right.

"Don't you dare ask me to tell you again what else Jackie said that day!" she threatened, sounding actually fierce. "Next time you get a cold, do not get it when somebody is going to make a speech on why she's proud she's Jewish. Or get up your nerve afterwards and ask her to tell you about it herself! That *is* a possibility."

Me ask Jacqueline Bernstein to tell me about her speech? Emily knew perfectly well that that was not a possibility, so there was no point in discussing it. Jackie is beautiful, rich, popular, and a year older than we are. She didn't get accelerated so she isn't ahead of us in school, but she is in a different class. We've never been in the same room.

Sheila—dear, dear Sheila—was the very first Jewish kid to be in the same class with me ever.

"Anyway, if you'd quit jumping on everything she does, Sheila's not so bad," Emily got back to the subject at hand. "I mean, she is bad. I grant you she is certainly far from good. But she's not a monster. Why can't you just make up your mind to ignore her?"

I muttered something between an "I don't know" and a "Yeah, okay." It was only a sound, not words. Suddenly, I felt tired, tired of Sheila's unreasonableness, tired of Emily's calm voice of reason, tired of myself somewhere in the middle. We trudged on in silence Emily finally broke it. I was ready for just about anything but what she said.

"There *are* prejudiced people, you know, Kate,"

she told me simply. "Maybe Sheila's prejudiced too—against people like you."

"People like me," I echoed blankly.

Emily hesitated for one split second. Then she blundered on bravely.

"Sort of half-and-half people. Neither one thing nor the other. You know exactly what I mean, Katharine Bloomfield, so stop pretending you don't."

Usually I would have fixed Emily Blair but fast for calling me a half-and-half person. But she was right, of course. I did know what she meant. I would have known right off except that, in that moment, I'd stumbled on a discovery.

"Sheila's Jewish." That was all Emily had said. And, for a couple of seconds (until she yelled at me) I'd actually thought she meant "Jewish people are all like Sheila." Talk about jumping to conclusions! What had I just said so self-righteously? I remembered. "She ought to be ready to give people a chance before she decides about them." That was some chance I'd given Emily! And Emily was my best friend. How could I have thought she meant something as stupid as that?

(Now I know. It wasn't Emily who was thinking stupid things. They were there in my own mind before Emily opened her mouth. But that afternoon, I wasn't ready to see into myself. Not that far anyway.)

"Okay," I said slowly. "I guess you could be right."

"You don't mean you have changed your mind about Sheila Rosenthal?" Emily raised her eyebrows at me and her mouth quirked up. I did sound extremely halfhearted. I had a lot to think about.

I scowled and then laughed.

"I still say she is horrible," I stated. "But maybe she has reasons. Just maybe, you understand. I really do not believe any reasons are good enough to explain away her rudeness and—"

Emily interrupted.

"Ah, but you will keep an open mind, won't you, Miss Bloomfield?" she teased, reminding me again of Dad.

"Well . . . I'll watch for signs of improvement. That much I'll do. I am not hopeful."

We had reached the Blairs' house. It is a small snug house tucked in between two big ones. I think of it as Louisa's house.

"Come on in and see her," invited my friend, reading my mind as usual.

Louisa Blair was seven months old then. I have not had much to do with babies, but those I have encountered have struck me as being a bit dull till they've learned to talk. Louisa was something else again. I'd waited for her to be born. She was my sister almost as much as she was Emily's. As a matter of fact, my own sister Marilyn doesn't count compared to Louisa.

I think one of the reasons she is so special to me is because I was left alone with her once, when she was almost brand new. I wrote her a poem about it. I've written other silly rhymes about her. I've shared those right away with Emily and Mrs. Blair. But this poem was just between Louisa and me. It was a long time before I could let Emily read it. (In the end, of course, I couldn't help myself. Back then we always read each other's poems.)

Louisa was six weeks old when I wrote it. Now, while Emily checked in with her mother, I went back over the words in my mind.

### Louisa, Louisa

My family is having dinner with the Blairs.
I come early.
Emily shows off Louisa.
Louisa, being just six weeks old,
    is not interested. She keeps falling asleep.
"Smile, Louisa," Emily orders,
    joggling her rudely. "Smile for Kate."
Louisa yawns,
Waves one fist haphazardly
    and firmly closes both eyes.
"Emily, come and help me put
    the leaf in the table," Mrs. Blair calls.
"Drat!" says Emily. She hands over the baby.
"Hold her," she commands, unnecessarily,
and disappears.
    So I hold you, Louisa.
    I sit very still and I hold you
        and watch you sleep.

For one moment, you are all mine.
Not that there is much of you.
But your eyelids flutter;
I can feel you breathing.
You are terribly alive, Louisa.

There is so much you do not know.
Louisa, you do not know about schools.
Do you know words yet, Louisa?
          No, no words.
You have never heard of computers.
You have never heard of dying, Louisa.
Shhh. Sleep.
You will discover the sun.
You will see Emily laughing.
You will come upon the alphabet
          and rainbows.
You will ride up an escalator.
You will read *The Secret Garden*
          for the first time.
You may go to Africa.
You'll get a letter.
You will wear shoes—
          and create a dance all your own.
Here is a secret, Louisa:
Living is worth schools;
Loving balances computers.
Even dying, Louisa,
          and knowing about dying,
          cannot stop your dancing.
But now I am holding you

And you are sleeping.
Louisa, shh.
I love you right now, Louisa,
            before you know anything,
Before you even know that you are Louisa.

"Is she *still* sleeping?" Emily asks,
            bouncing back into the room.
Sometimes Emily is an awfully noisy girl.

I was remembering that Louisa when Emily brought the new Louisa out and plunked her into my arms. It wasn't such an honor now to hold her. Not to Emily, at least.

"She weighs a ton," she complained.

Louisa made a happy little snorting noise and pounded my shoulder with her fist.

"Quit that," I told her, laughing.

"Mother says, will you stay for supper?" Emily said.

I nodded.

"That's what I already told her," said Emily smugly. "But listen. Let's make up our minds to one thing, Katharine."

"What one thing is that?" I asked, tickling Louisa and listening to her wonderful explosions of giggles.

"We will *not* talk about Sheila Rosenthal," Emily decreed.

But of course we did.

# 6

# Cramps

Such a huge, confusing mishmash of people it all is, as I try to get straight what happened. Susannah, the Sutherlands, all our parents, Emily and Louisa, David Nelson and Lindsay. Only Lin and Dave really played no part, no important part. Neither did the Sutherlands, I guess. And Louisa matters only because Louisa matters always.

Yet, somehow, Louisa is in it. She will not be two years old for another five months almost, so she did not have a starring role with lines to say. But she was there with Susannah at the center. That poem I wrote for her—it haunted me. It sounds crazy to be haunted by one of your own poems but I began to be. At the oddest times, I would find myself thinking about the words and about the small "terribly alive" person I had held.

Louisa would grow up. She would see Emily laughing. And she would see me too—Kate Bloomfield.

Who was I?

Suppose she asked me someday "What do you mean, Kate Bloomfield? What do you mean, 'loving balances computers'?" What would I answer?

Well, I knew she wasn't going to ask. She might want me to read her a story. She'd need me to help her tie her shoes maybe. She'd ask for a cookie. But not about loving or living. Still, I began looking around sort of, hoping to find an answer.

Maybe, if I listened, Dad would give it to me in one of his quotes. There were enough of them, that's for sure. He quotes somebody at least once in every waking hour.

It used to drive me insane.

If he'd only just do it at home, I'd moan to myself. Or even if he did it at the store too—but not in front of my friends.

He has this special look on his face when he quotes, a look of being positive you'll see how perfectly these words fit what has happened. My friends did not see. Ever!

Then, one day, this changed. Emily got one. It wasn't a hard one, not if you are an addict of

*Charlotte's Web*, like Emily. Just the same, it was really something.

She and I were sitting around talking about away back when we first made friends and then discovered we both wrote poems. Dad was there, waiting to eat, and suddenly, he smiled at the two of us and came out with: "'It is not often that someone comes along who is a true friend and a good writer.'"

For an instant, there was the funniest look on Emily's face—as though she'd just discovered she'd lost a tooth—startled and searching. Then, well, her face lit up. Brighter than any candle. Like a whole bonfire.

"'Charlotte was both,'" she quoted back at him, smooth as cream.

They beamed at each other. You could tell they felt like the smartest people in the entire world. And I beamed too, insanely. I knew then that I didn't want him changed.

Oh, I still moaned—but I listened too. Without admitting it even to myself, I began to enjoy him.

But he didn't come up with any pat answers to my questions.

Meanwhile, Sheila and I continued to be at daggers drawn. Well, it wasn't quite that out in the open. We had an armed truce going. We did not speak. We didn't seem to see each other. I had no idea what was bugging her but I wasn't taking any chances.

Myself, I did come closer to understanding.

When I started being honest, it wasn't all that complicated. I had felt more or less alone in my Jewishness for most of my life. It hadn't been important, and yet it had. Like the language you speak isn't what's most significant about you. It doesn't decide the kind of person you are going to be, for instance. But it is part of you. You belong with other people who speak French or whatever.

I belonged with my father—except it was vague, not something we talked about, just something we knew.

Once in awhile, my parents would joke about themselves and their marriage. Once in awhile, Dad would tell stories of when he was a little boy and I'd look into a world different from mine. But he did not tell many stories. And always, afterwards, he was haunted by a sadness.

This sadness in him was beginning to bother me. I had grown up with it and so, till recently, had accepted it without question. I had learned how to sidestep it often—when to start him on a new track so that he would not draw away from us into aloneness. I knew what was likely to bring it on. I knew all about it except why.

Why was really none of my business, I guess. But Dad was the sensible one in our family. Mother and I went off on tangents, got churned up over nothing, made snap judgments and lost our tempers. He stayed reasonable, relaxed, ready to laugh. He kept us on a more or less even keel. Only this one thing, talking about his boyhood, changed him. Only this one thing made him close a door within and slap up a **DO NOT ENTER** sign.

You'd think anybody should be allowed one thing to be unreasonable about. And, if the stories had been sad, I'd have understood. That was what baffled me, though. The stories were not sad.

How could they be, with Bess in all of them!

My grandmother Bess (Dad called her Bess himself half the time when he talked about her) was a person who lighted up the world around her. When I was small, I used to press Dad for more stories about her and ask again and again for ones I especially loved.

They all took place before I was born. Some had happened before my father himself was born. But I knew the Bess I met in them almost as well as I knew Emily Blair.

Bess's naming the chairs was one of my favorites.

*Her* childhood had been hard. Her parents had come to Canada as immigrants, without a cent to spare. They hoped to make their fortunes, according to Dad, but at first they were dogged with bad luck. Their lack of English was against them. My great-grandfather became ill. It was a bad time. Only Bess managed to enjoy living.

She was three when they came. When she was six, she could talk English as easily as Polish.

She learned to read right off the bat. Then she wanted books of her own and she wanted a doll.

There was no money for dolls or for books. Her mother was too hard pressed to make a doll. Maybe she just didn't know how.

Most children would have nagged and nagged until they were finally forced to give up. Not Bess! When she saw she would get no doll, she made her own dolls out of their three straight-backed kitchen chairs. She played with them by the hour, giving each a distinct personality. One was always a little girl her own age.

"She claimed they even had the same birth-day," Dad told me.

The other two changed their characters depending on the game. Sometimes they were parents. Sometimes, witches. Sometimes, younger children.

My great-grandmother (she stays shadowy in my mind, stern and tired and without a name) worried over Bess and those chairs.

"She was certain I was possessed," Bess told her own children.

In spite of that, the little girl went right on moving her friends around, making them talk to each other, scolding them, putting them to bed, and doing all the things with them that another child would have needed a doll for.

"What was the girl-chair's name?" I used to ask over and over. I knew but I wanted to hear it once more, to be certain.

"Rosegay," Dad said.

"Where did she find that name?" I wanted to know.

Dad shook his head.

"Bess had her head full of stories, her own and other people's," he said. "She could invent anything. I don't know where any of it came from or how she kept it, married to my father. He never understood her nonsense, although I think he warmed his hands at it just as Abby and I did."

The silence came then. I was outside. But I had lots to think about. I was still too young to care.

I tried naming a doll Rosegay after Bess's girl-chair. It didn't work. That chair was too real, too alive. The name belonged to her and her alone. I didn't play with dolls much. Some, of course. But not a lot. They seemed tame.

Bess was still Bess when she became my father's mother. She even played elaborate jokes on her children. Maybe "jokes" isn't the right word. She told them, for instance, that they had an older brother who had run away to sea. Micah, his name was.

"The adventures she dreamed up for that Micah!" Dad would say, laughing. "Pirates, he fought. Countries never heard of before or since, he discovered. Finally, when Abby and I were popeyed with excitement, it would be too much for Father. 'Bess, enough now!' he would thunder. We'd be believing every word of it till that moment. Then we would shriek at her 'It's not true! It's not true!' 'Micah not true?' she would say, her eyes wide with innocence. 'Why, he's the image of your father.'"

Dad would laugh again, remembering. And I would laugh too, wishing I still had this wonderful relative.

"She's the one you get your way with words from," Dad would tell me.

It was all so happy, so good. Yet, minutes later, the sadness would creep in, baffling me, and at last making me stop asking him to go on and tell me more.

She was Jewish, though, my grandmother Bess. That much was certain. And so was I. Even though the books I read seemed to say you got your religion from your mother. Even though once, when I asked Dad outright "Am I Jewish?" he could only tell me "That is something you'll spend your whole life finding out, Katharine."

What Dad and the books both overlooked was that, if you were not Jewish, you had to be something else. That is the way things work. And I wasn't anything. I didn't fit.

Not fitting can mean you are free—but not when you've had no choice. I guess that is what I'm stammering around about. I looked down at Louisa sleeping in my arms; I watched my father sit with a book open in front of him, not reading, just being alone; I stared across at Sheila Rosenthal scowling over her math.

And I began to want to know what everything meant and why I was here.

Then, one morning in science class, Sheila made a peculiar noise. I glanced over at her automatically. I sit right opposite her. I couldn't help looking. She was exactly the color of cream of mushroom soup.

"What's the matter?" I asked.

I didn't shout but I didn't precisely whisper either. The way she was sitting, sort of hunched over, and her face that color—I was scared.

She glared at me. It was a pretty feeble glare but I recognized it for what it was. She almost wished I'd mind my own business, except she was feeling too terrible.

"Cramps," she ground out through clenched teeth.

I hesitated, not knowing what move to make next. I looked at the other two girls who shared our table. Jan Wellington and Marnie Walters. They were as thick as thieves. Jan *was* a thief if you believed the rumors. She has the reputation of being the best shoplifter in our school. Marnie is a follower and a sort of pale snob. She hasn't enough character to be a really good snob and put her whole heart into it. She just kind of sidesteps everything and says "Uh . . . I don't know . . ." and fades out.

Marnie was very busy fading out right then.

I wanted Emily, but Emily takes geography when I take science.

"Hey, Jan," I muttered, "Sheila needs help."

Jan was busy. She was making a complicated diagram. She shrugged.

"You're elected," she said, and kept right on drawing.

Sheila wouldn't want help from me, no matter what. That much I was still certain of. I looked further afield. Surely there was somebody . . .

Everywhere I turned, I met the same blank stare. This was up to me. Sheila was mine.

I didn't understand right away.

And the funny thing is, maybe I never *did* understand. But, all at once, I thought I did. Sheila was Jewish; so was I. Let us look out for each other.

I was furious—and not with Sheila, for a change.

Okay, I thought, if that's the way you want it, that's just how it'll be. Watch!

That was the first time I ever thought of the other kids as "you" like that. As though I weren't one of them. I was crazy. Nobody liked Sheila. I already knew that. She hadn't tried to be liked, not by the kids in our class. Her friends *were* Jewish kids—Jackie Bernstein and Sheldon Gagen and Jeanette Spiegel. At least, I'd never seen her hanging around with anyone else. And there she was, right at my table. Why should the entire class rise up on her behalf when I was sitting not three feet from her? It wouldn't have made sense if they had. For that matter, most of them probably hadn't noticed yet that anything was wrong.

None of this was clear to me then. I was too outraged, too much the mother tiger. Sheila needed me! And suddenly, she was my own, mine to protect, mine to rescue. Let somebody try to interfere, that was all!

"Do you want to leave?" I asked softly, not looking at anybody else any longer. "Do you want to go home?"

She nodded. Her straggly hair plopped forward limply over her cheeks, like a little kid's does. She looked too miserable to move.

I subsided for one instant and just sat. I had better wait for her to revive; wait for her to realize she was talking to me, Kate; wait for the old Sheila to come up fighting.

She did not stir except to huddle her elbows in closer to herself.

Someone had to get her excused.

"Why me?" I asked silently as I got to my feet. I went to the front of the room and told Mr. Clark. He blushed. "Of course, of course," he whispered very fast.

What a science teacher!

I returned to the table.

"It's okay. You can go," I told Sheila.

She did not move. I am not sure she even heard. Her eyes were half shut. She appeared ready to flop over in a faint. I reached out a quick hand to keep her upright. She did not draw away.

"You'd better go with her, Kate," Jan said.

She had emerged from her diagram and looked as concerned as I imagine she has it in her to look. Marnie, of course, came in with "Yeah, you'd better."

I didn't argue. Some of the boys were beginning to stare now. Also Mr. Clark was so nervous it was pathetic.

"Come on!" I said and cupped my hand around Sheila's elbow.

She has bony elbows. She felt fragile. She isn't, but that is how she felt at that moment. (Sheila is actually strung together out of piano wire and whalebone or something equally indestructible.)

I more or less hoisted her down off the lab stool. She came without one word. Together, we made our way along the back wall and out the classroom door. I was taking her to the Office.

I still did not believe any of it.

# 7

# Another Rosenthal
# is heard from

Sheila and I did not scurry. She kind of hobbled along, bending over. She continued to lean on me. As we progressed, she felt less and less fragile.

I thought of Little Lord Fauntleroy. I loved that nutty book to pieces when I was about nine. I remember wondering what it would be like to call your mother "Dearest" all the time. I did *not* try it on Mother. I knew better.

"Just lean on me, Grandfather," I murmured, imagining, for one instant, that Sheila was the gouty Earl of Dorrincourt.

Sheila didn't hear—or didn't care, if she did.

At last, we reached the Office. I eased the kid into a chair and went to get the secretary to phone for somebody. Mrs. Rosenthal was out.

"Don't you worry," Miss Agnew fluted, waving me away. "I'll find someone. You just take care of your little friend."

My little friend indeed! Miss Agnew is a prize example of what the generation gap is all about.

I did wait with Sheila. What else could I do? That outer office was so busy. Typewriters clicked along like mad and went *bing*! People kept arriving and leaving with memos and mail. An electrician was doing something to a light switch in one corner and, while he worked, he whistled through his teeth. Nobody paid any attention to us. Nobody.

"As lonely as hell!" That's an expression my mother uses. I now have a picture of hell. It's a huge office full of people with nobody listening to anybody.

Then Sheila's father arrived!

People listened after that, I'm telling you. He bombed in there. *Wham!* The door swung back and crashed. It is one of those crashless type doors, but Dr. Rosenthal made it shiver. He only wasted half a sentence on Miss Agnew.

"Where's my—?"

He saw us and wheeled away from the desk. Miss Agnew's mouth opened and shut a couple of times but no sound came. She looked like a goldfish.

Now you would have thought Dr. Rosenthal

would have been one person who should have understood how things were with Sheila. By that time, she had started looking gray and wobbly. She reminded me of the paste we used to use in first grade. And he *is* a doctor! Ear, nose and throat, though. Maybe that makes a difference. Maybe he's forgotten about everything lower than the neck.

"All right, Sheila," he barked, as though she'd had nerve enough to say something—she hadn't. "I'm only halfway through making rounds and I have an office full of work waiting. Let's GO!"

I don't know what I thought would happen, what I imagined she'd do. In her place, I hope I would have thrown a tantrum at least.

Sheila—nasty, mean, always top-dog Sheila—simply got up and, head down, went staggering meekly toward the door.

Cowed at last! Finally put in her place! I should have been cheering.

I could have killed him. I was so mad I think I could have killed every father in the world, mine included. I leaped up, ran two steps, caught up with Sheila and grabbed hold of her again. I put my arm right around her, all the way. I clutched her!

I had plenty of time. The bell had rung for lunch while we were waiting. I'd go home with her, if I had to. I'd put her to bed. I'd get her aspirins and a glass of water. I'd find her a heating pad. I'd fix him.

I hate bullies.

"Who are you?" Dr. Rosenthal asked, finally noticing me.

He couldn't have missed me really. I had his daughter tightly grasped under my wing and I was marching her along not two feet from him.

"I am Katharine Bloomfield," I answered.

I was not polite. The words were okay but the tone was something else. Also I did not turn my head. Still, out of the corner of my eye, I could see his lips twitch. But he couldn't have smiled.

"Nate Bloomfield's daughter?"

"My father is Jonathan Bloomfield," I acknowledged.

I tried to sound like Catherine the Great talking to a serf. I felt willing and ready for total war. Let him say one wrong word about my father. Just let him try!

He went right ahead and did.

"I should have guessed," he said. "You're just like him—thinking yourself a cut above the rest of the world and not caring who knows it."

I did not even take in the fact that he was insulting me. Shocked words leaped out of me. But I kept my hold on Sheila, shock or no shock.

"My father is *not* like that! He isn't. He doesn't think he's better than anybody—"

"Good. Fine," Dr. Rosenthal cut in smoothly. "Because he isn't. Never has been. You can tell him I said so."

Then he took Sheila from me, swiftly and expertly, as though she were a parcel and he a postman. Without a word to her, he stowed her tidily away in the back seat of his car. Before I could gather breath for a counterattack, he was behind the wheel. The motor roared.

"He IS special!" I yelled then, outraged.

"He has a loyal daughter anyway," he shot back, over the noise of the engine. "Good-bye Florence Nightingale! And thank you." He waved. They were gone.

I stood there stupidly, not sure what had happened. Then I came around. I was fuming. I was sorry for Sheila. And I was utterly bewildered. It had all happened so fast. I must have imagined part of it.

Except I knew I hadn't. When he had waved, his face—thin, sharp, and unlike Sheila's—had been friendly, amused. It couldn't have been, yet it was. I could still see the laughter in his eyes.

He knows Dad, I thought.

That much I had understood. He knew Dad and didn't like him any more than I liked Sheila.

Yet there had been something more complicated in his voice when he spoke of my father. And he had meant that smile.

If I'm like my father, Sheila's like hers, I decided, turning to go in.

Only my father was not the way Dr. Rosenthal said he was. At least, not with me.

And neither had Sheila been like Sheila. She

was so, so quiet. When I had held her against me, she had sort of shrunk. Oh, that doesn't tell it. She had seemed without armor—and I had thought Sheila never went unguarded.

Tomorrow things would be changed between us. I did not know quite how. I was not exactly eager to find out. But when you've leaned on somebody like that, or let somebody lean on you, things are not the same afterwards. You can't stand completely apart from that person again.

Even if you both want to.

We *would* both want to. She did not like me any more now than she had before. If anything, she had added reason to dislike me, for I'd seen the way her father treated her. Well, I did not like her or her smart-aleck father either. We were even, there.

I tramped down the hall. I wanted her out of my mind. Out!

She was so quiet though.

I thought about punching his teeth in. Not seriously. Just a passing thought, but I enjoyed it.

I wondered suddenly what her mother was like. I had a queer feeling I was going to find that out too.

I reached the door of our homeroom. I stopped. I glanced around. Nobody was near enough to hear me.

"Sheila Rosenthal," I said softly, "take yourself and your whole dumb family and *drop dead in unison.* Who cares about you anyway? Who *cares?*"

I knew the answer. I didn't understand it. It was the craziest thing I had ever heard of. We had nothing in common. Nothing!

"Not one single solitary thing!" I said louder than I meant to, startling myself.

So why? Why did I care? Because I did. And I knew it.

I felt shaken and bruised by all that had happened that morning. As I opened the door and went in to lunch, I also felt doomed.

# 8

# At the store

If I were making all this up out of my head, now would be the time when I would finally come to realize Sheila was misunderstood, and she and I would become kindred spirits and I would help her to get her life smoothed out. But I'm not making it up, and that isn't what happened. What really happened is much more unexpected and harder to figure out. Still, that is what I set out to do—figure it out. And the first step is remembering. It isn't simple.

Once, for about two days, my mother took up weaving. She came home with a table loom and instructions and lots of yarn and told us she had decided she needed something she could do with her hands, to relax with in the evenings after work. I sat by, fascinated, while she struggled to set the thing up and thread it. Dad didn't say much. Mother began to weave. It didn't last. I have never seen a wilder mess than her try at making a simple scarf. Or maybe it was a placemat.

"But what's wrong, April?" Dad asked her.

"There are far too many threads!" she wailed.

She went back to reading books and we all breathed a sigh of relief.

I know now what she meant. There are so many threads in what I am trying to put together. I struggle to hold onto them all, to make sure each comes into the pattern when it should and does what it is supposed to do, but the dark strips are too wide, and then I forget a color altogether. It is bumpy too, and there are gaps you can see through. Still, that was the way of it. Uneven. I didn't know, as I went through the days, raging and calming down, laughing and writing poems, making discoveries and forgetting things I already knew, that in the end I'd be looking for a pattern.

Already, I think I am beginning to see one. Or am I? It is never neat, never clear. But then, I wouldn't want life tidy—one color from first to last. I like surprises.

Those days were full of surprises.

I became obsessed with the Rosenthals. I didn't like Sheila but I could not shut up about her. Emily began to grit her teeth whenever I started.

"Not again!" she said. "Please, please, not today."

For a couple of days after that, I managed not to mention her, but there were some deafening silences so I gave that up. It was better to bore Emily and madden her than to have things unsaid between us, I thought. I imagined Emily thought so too.

"She did it!" I rejoiced one afternoon. "Sheila finally beat us in English!"

We had been given an essay to write, a research essay. Emily and I are not mad about research.

"I'm still better at writing than she is and so are you," snapped Emily.

"I know that," I told her, startled at the venom in her voice. "It's just that her father's so . . . so . . . well, I just know it will be important to her to tell him she came out on top."

Emily did not unbend.

"My father wants me to get good marks too," she said. "I thought you didn't like Sheila?"

"I don't," I said.

I know now she didn't really believe me. Not having encountered Dr. Rosenthal, how could she understand my sudden sympathy for a girl I claimed not to like? I wouldn't have wished Dr. Rosenthal on my worst enemy—and whatever Emily thought, Sheila was still just that.

April warmed into May. I baby-sat. I read poetry. I kept watching for Susannah.

I saw her twice.

The first time, she was, once again, in the

distance. We were both on our way to school and I glimpsed her down a side street. She was skipping. Not with a rope. Hippety-hopping. Whenever I picture Susannah, even now, I see her moving. She always seems to be more than half flying, because she goes with such freedom and grace.

The other time, I came on Jean Sutherland and her, playing together in the Sutherlands' yard.

"Susannah!" I cried.

I was so pleased to have found her, so eager to ask her sensible, grown-up questions like "Where do you live?" and stuff. It didn't work out that way.

"I am not Susannah," she said gravely. "I am Dorothy. I just got here from Kansas."

For one instant, I didn't catch on. Then, in the nick of time, I found the right words.

"Where's Toto?" I asked.

"Would you like to be Toto?"

Dorothy's eyes glowed. Jean, who turned out to be The Tin Woodman, the Cowardly Lion, and the Scarecrow in one, protested.

"She's too big, Susan."

"I don't think so," Susannah said. She smiled up at me. "We need a few witches too," she added.

Before we were finished, I even had a turn at being Ozma. It was terrific. There were just the three of us. I felt I'd come back into a kingdom, a kingdom I'd been exiled from without my even having noticed, a kingdom I hadn't exactly missed but which felt like home.

I did not find out anything sensible about Susannah. They were still playing when I had to go. I'd been helping out at the store and letting Mother go home an hour early. I didn't exactly have to. Dad could get along without me. But I made things easier and I knew he liked having me there. I was beginning to know what I was doing too.

That was where I met Sheila's mother.

It was almost time to close. Well, past time really, but I wasn't saying anything. I was hungry so I was wishing Dad would hurry but I knew better than to tell him so. If I had, he'd have launched into a lecture about not letting time be your master. Next thing, he'd be telling me about Walden Pond again, an extra half hour would have gone by, and Mother would be phoning to see what had happened to us.

Then, all of a sudden, I came up with a poem of my own. Some of my poems take time but others simply arrive. Bang! A poem! This one was like that and it made me feel terrific. It was crazy, all right, but so what? I grabbed up my clipboard and scribbled it down, forgetting Dad and time and everything.

### I Said to the World

I said to the world,
"Here I am—I, Kate Bloomfield."
But the world paid no attention.

I said to the world,
"Hey, world, I'm here!
Don't you understand?
I, Kate Bloomfield, have arrived."
The world ignored me.
I took myself away into a corner.
And whispered, "Guess what? I'm here.
You know—Kate Bloomfield?"
My self yelled right out loud
"YeeaaaAAAY KATE!"
And spun six cartwheels
Up the middle of Main Street.
The world turned.
"What did you say?" asked the world.
But I paid no attention.
After all, I gave it its chance.
If it missed me,
It has only itself to blame.

I sat grinning at the words. They sprawled
across the page, laughing. For that one instant, I
felt sure of who I was. I knew I mattered. I had
all the answers. And I loved the power of being
myself and nobody else.

Then the door opened.

I had forgotten it was past closing time. I'm
sure Dad had too. I don't think Mrs. Rosenthal
had any idea how late it was. She walked in and
right across the floor to where my father stood
behind the counter. Before she said one word, I
knew they knew each other—had known each

other for a long time. Later, I remembered that Dr. Rosenthal knew Dad too. I'd meant to ask him about it but I never had. Partly I'd forgotten; partly I'd been scared somehow. Maybe I didn't want to meet the "Nate Bloomfield" Dr. Rosenthal had talked about.

"Hello, Jonathan," this woman said.

I still had no notion who she was, of course. I did notice that she called him Jonathan. People call my father by so many different names that I've grown interested in keeping track. Mother almost always calls him Slim. She's the only one who does. (He isn't. He's the opposite, if anything.) She does call him Jon too, and once in a blue moon, Jonathan. Lots of people call him Jonathan. His sister called him Nathan. I know because that is what she always says in his stories. They both had long names and shortened them. Abigail, hers was. She's Abby in the stories.

This strange woman, who knew my father, did not wait for him to say hello back. She turned right away to me.

"And you're Kate," she said. "You look like a Kate."

I didn't know what that was supposed to mean but I smiled at her. She has that kind of warmth in her face. You can't help smiling back.

Except my father seemed to be doing a pretty good job of not smiling.

"What are you doing in here, Elsa?" he asked.

She made a face at him, crinkled up her nose. He did sound rude.

"If you're in that kind of a mood, Kate can help me," she shrugged off his lack of welcome, turning to me. "Where'll I find that programmed math book Sheila saw you working on?"

I knew then. I mean, there's only one Sheila! My eyes—well, I stared.

She looks like a mother, I thought, in that instant.

My mother doesn't. She's too pretty, and her clothes are too bright and up to date. Also, she clowns in an unmotherly way. Mrs. Rosenthal was short, only not too, and kind of round and rumpled. Her hair had lots of gray in it and her face looked as though she'd been laughing all her life. How on earth did Sheila belong to this mother?

"Don't plotz, Kate, and shut your mouth. You look foolish," Mrs. Rosenthal said lightly. "Now— the book? Or must I search the premises?"

I came to, slid off the stool where I'd been perched and ran to get it for her. (Ours is the only store in town that carries it. Poor Sheila!) Mrs. Rosenthal paid Dad for the book. They said something more, nothing important. But Dad did seem to have lowered his defenses. He sounded normal again.

Then, suddenly, she barged right in. It was as though she saw the door clearly marked NO ADMITTANCE but could not help herself. I had seen the door too. It was that barrier of sadness and something more that came between my father and me, shutting me outside. I resented it. I feared it. But I had learned not to intrude.

Mrs. Rosenthal was made of sterner stuff.

"Your sister needs you, Jonathan," she said.

"I'm right here. She knows where to find me," Dad slammed back.

The words were so hard you could almost see them.

Mrs. Rosenthal threw those words aside as though they barely touched her—no, as though she refused to let them hurt.

"Does Kate even know she has a grandfather?" she asked.

The abrupt question was directed at Dad but she was watching me as she spoke. My astonished face was answer enough.

"And a cousin," she swept on. "You must go, Jon, for that boy's sake. Abby should never have moved back in with your father. You *do* know that's where they are? . . . All right. All right. So I'm leaving. Sam forbade me to come, if that helps. I've said what I came to say, and I'm glad. Go, Jonathan. Go to them."

She smiled at me again.

"Bye, Kate," she said.

She tried to speak lightly at the last but I saw, in that second, that her eyes were filled with tears. I did not understand any of it. But I wanted to cry too.

Right then, some of what most bugged me about Sheila . . . well, anyway, I liked her mother.

Dad went on putting things away after the door shut behind her. He said nothing to me. I sat still and tried to be invisible. It is something I've always wanted to be able to do. I never have wanted it more than right at that moment.

As I perched there, breathing as soundlessly as I could, wishing I could hush my heartbeat somehow, I glanced down and saw my own new poem, the letters dashing boldly across the open page. It seemed three hundred years since I'd written it.

That Kate was gone. There was not a yell left in me. I knew only one thing, that my father was closed away from me in a lonely place. Maybe it was a place he had made for himself. Mrs. Rosenthal seemed to think so. She talked as though he had only to turn the key and open the door. I did not know. I just wanted to go to him, to bring him comfort.

But there was no way in.

# 9

# Parts of the puzzle

C RASH!

I knew what had happened before I looked up. Dad had been predicting it for the past week—only he said Mother was going to be the one to do it. He'd bought a tall, thin swiveling bookrack to fill in one unused corner at the store. Ever since he'd set it up, we'd been reaching out and catching it just in time. It was so light and unsteady that you couldn't give it a good twirl without it swaying perilously.

"It's more worry than it's worth," Dad had said that afternoon. "I'll move it out first thing tomorrow before one of you *does* send it over and we find ourselves knee-deep in Penguins."

Now Father stood ankle-deep in Penguin Books and swore. He doesn't swear often but when he does, there's no mistaking it. I started to go to his rescue.

"Stay where you are," he barked at me, over his shoulder. "There isn't room for the two of us here. I'll move this thing out right now and just stack the books in the back room till I find a better place for them."

It wasn't that crowded really but I didn't argue. I sat back and tried not to think of Mother. We'd be at least another half hour. At least! Supper would be burned to a cinder.

If she'd started supper, that is. There was a good chance she had become involved in something else and forgotten all about us. On the other hand, every so often, without warning, she goes in for a cooking orgy. Herbs and all. When April cooks, she likes you to eat it promptly. "A woman of extremes," Dad calls her.

He sounds despairing but actually he's proud of her. They are great believers in freedom, even when it is downright inconvenient. As Mother says, "There's always lots of bread and cheese." It is fortunate that all three of us are fond of bread and cheese.

Either way, there wasn't a heck of a lot I could do. If she had cooked, she'd cooked.

I slouched over with one elbow on the counter. I'd ducked out of worrying about

Mother nicely and I wasn't worried about Dad any longer either. While he could swear like that, he didn't need me brooding over him. I could devote some thought to my newly discovered relatives.

A cousin! A grandfather!

Dad had started dismantling the bookrack now. I might as well risk one more try while he had his back turned. I slid off the stool, scooped up an armload of books and started for the back room. He didn't say a word.

When I'd cleared the floor completely, he was still working on the bookrack, doing a thorough job of it. He obviously intended to return it whence it came.

I went back to my stool and my thoughts.

The aunt was Abby, of course. There had only been the two of them.

And Micah, I thought, with a quick smile for Bess.

She and Micah still meant far more to me than these faceless relations Mrs. Rosenthal had come up with.

When I was Susannah's age, I had believed Uncle Micah was real—or I told myself I did, anyway. I wanted relatives. Everybody I knew seemed to have dozens of them. My parents and Marilyn didn't measure up to droves of aunts, uncles, cousins, and grandparents. So, for awhile, I dreamed of the day when my sailor uncle would come home.

"Micah!" Dad would gasp, staring at the stranger. "But I thought she made you up!"

I knew how this uncle looked. Exactly like Uncle Alec in *Eight Cousins*. Tall and brown, with bright blue eyes and curly hair. He liked girls, me especially (he ignored Marilyn), and he brought me a monkey from far away, a monkey for my own.

Over and over, on the way home from school, I'd promise myself that if I didn't step on a single crack or if I walked backwards the whole way or if I hopped on every third step, today would be the day. I'd open the door and he'd be there, waiting. He never was, but expecting him was exciting enough.

I had, long ago, given up this daydream. But I still loved the runaway Micah and wished he were real, just as Dad and Abby had done.

Or had my aunt loved him?

I didn't really know her that well. I pieced together scraps of talk. She was serious. Once Dad had said "Mother often seemed more my age than Abby did." And another time, "Abby could never see a joke. She used to laugh but she always laughed a little late."

She was like Grandfather while Dad was like Bess. Had he told me that? No. But I was sure I was right.

Suddenly, a voice deep within me cried out in rebellion, "They're dead though! They must be. Otherwise he would have said something! She has to be wrong, Sheila's mother."

Yet I knew it was the voice that was wrong.

None of Dad's stories were finished. Abby was twenty-two when he left home. She never grew any older. Till now I had assumed she was dead, but why would she be dead at twenty-two?

I figured it out. She would be fifty now. Abby—fifty! And this grandfather, Bess's husband—why, he would be over eighty!

"She was so much younger," I could hear Dad saying. "Eleven years! I think her parents arranged the match although she never said. He waited, though, till his printing business was making a clear profit and he had a house bought and furnished before he married her. She used to tease him about the way he kept her waiting. She even teased him about his age—and he let her. Abby and I could never understand how she dared. 'Children, be still!' she'd order us. 'Your aged father is about to hand down some of his wisdom!'"

My father left that story unended. I never learned what his father had said. I saw only Bess, her hands folded respectfully, her mouth prim, her eyes dancing with mockery. And, in spite of what my father left unsaid, I felt a deep bond between this stern man and his young laughing wife.

I straightened. Had I made a discovery? I thought perhaps I had. Oh, not the love between my grandparents. That I had always known. But about Dad and Grandfather. I checked back through years of conversations.

Why, I knew no stories about my grandfather at all. Not one. He was only there because Dad had to talk about Bess and he had been unable to talk about the one without the other. Grandfather was a figure in the background always. Bess had been the one Dad loved.

My father had disappeared into the back of the store now, taking the dismantled bookrack with him. I tried to imagine not loving him. It was impossible. Even when I was mad at him, he was like part of myself. If Grandfather had been cruel . . . but I knew he hadn't. Bess would not have teased a cruel man. And if Bess loved him, Dad must have loved him too.

He was scared of him, I reminded myself.

That did not change things. Love could be mixed up and still be love.

"Something must have happened," I whispered.

But what? Not death. Mrs. Rosenthal had made that much clear.

Bess had died. I did know that. I let go wondering about my father and his father and remembered instead the night Dad had told me about Bess's dying. Strange! That should have been the one really sad story. But it hadn't been. There had been no barrier between us that night.

Harold Whitely's mother had died suddenly. I didn't know her, and Harold was only one of the kids at school, nobody special. He had red hair and he bragged a lot. Still he was somebody my age exactly, somebody I had known since kindergarten. And his mother was dead.

I struggled not to stare at him when he came back to class after the funeral. I was nine or ten. I didn't want to, but I couldn't stop myself thinking about it. All at once, my mother was capable of dying and leaving me. I started to have nightmares.

Mother came in to me the first time it happened. I clung to her, sobbing wildly "You're alive! You're still here!" It didn't take her long to get the whole story from me. Then she washed my face, put me firmly back on my pillow, and told me dryly that she felt good for another fifty years or so and to stop worrying.

"When the time comes, you'll probably be glad to get rid of me," she laughed.

It should have helped, I guess. It didn't. The dreams came again, the next night and the next.

The fourth time, Dad came instead. He sat on the edge of my bed in the darkness. I could just see him in the light from the streetlamp outside. He did not make light of my fears. He did not even try to comfort me. He told me about Bess.

"I couldn't believe she was seriously ill," he said. "She was still so gay, so much herself. But she got thinner and thinner till a wind could have blown her away. Finally, I had to believe it. I was only a boy and I suppose she could read it in my face. Everybody else was pretending she would get well. I stopped saying anything."

"Was she in the hospital?" I gulped, coming out of the panic that followed my dream.

"No. She had been, but there was nothing more they could do for her so they let her come home. Her closest friend was a nurse. All her friends helped. The house seemed full of kindly, pitying women. Anyway, one evening, she told them all to go and have a rest, that I would stay with her for a little.

"They didn't want to go, I remember, and I was afraid to stay alone with her but she had her way. People always did what Bess told them to. Even Father. She made the decisions and then saw to it he gave the orders . . . Katharine?"

"Yes," I said.

He took my hand. I was calmer by this time, just listening to him. I waited for him to ask me if I was understanding what he was telling me but he just went on.

"She knew I was afraid, of course. You couldn't fool Bess. She said something silly first. I don't know what it was now but she made me laugh. I was astonished to hear myself laughing.

"Then she said, 'Nathan, I want to tell you something and I want you to remember it.' She held my hand the way I'm holding yours and she talked quietly. 'Life is good,' she said. 'Oh there are bad times but there is such joy, so many surprises. Even now, I enjoy so much. Being here with you, talking together this way, is so great a thing—it is like a gift.'"

Dad stopped but only for an instant.

"She asked me to make her a promise then, Katharine. 'Promise me that you will try to live every day you are alive,' she said.

"I did not know what she meant but I promised. And in the days that were left, I learned what she meant. She loved someone, gave to someone, laughed at something every day that she could . . . Katharine, I'm not asking you to promise me anything but I want you to try to catch her vision of life."

His hand was warm and steady on mine. I did not understand much more than that. But something of her courage reached me and I'll always remember what she said to him. I amazed myself by yawning suddenly.

"Okay. I'll try," I said, around the yawn.

He laughed.

"Go to sleep, child," he said.

I fell asleep almost at once. The nightmare did not come again.

When his mother died Dad was seventeen. He stayed at home for two more years. Abby helped him save enough money to leave when he was nineteen. He met Mother and there were lots of stories about the two of them and their early adventures and misadventures together. Nothing more about his family. Nothing at all.

Had Mother met them? Did they know about Marilyn and me?

I had a hundred questions. But no answers. None. And I could not ask.

"If Sheila knows, I hate her!" I told myself.

Then I grinned. What was I saying? That otherwise I liked her?

Dad turned. I fought to erase all expression from my face but I could feel the questions in my eyes. I looked hard at a book on a rack near me. It was something about Civilization and the Middle Ages. I don't suppose he was fooled.

"I'm ready now," my father said.

I followed him out the door. As he locked it, I thought of Sheila again.

Too chicken to come in and ask for her own math book, I jeered inwardly.

For no sane reason, that made me feel better.

# 10

# Emily and I do not fight

The next night, I wrote my "Alone" poem. I don't need to explain it. It explains itself. But I think it was then that I began to . . . began to what? I don't know. I sure as heck wasn't finding myself the way those teen-age books say. Yet it was something like that. Looking for myself is more like it, maybe.

### Alone

I am alone, and lonely.

My sadness makes everything around me
more beautiful.

The dusk falls softly,
As simply as a page turning
Or a bird lighting on the ground.
The sky glows dull-rose over the rooftops
And, high above me, a deep sea-blue-green.
I am caught up in it all—and small.
I search for words.
I ache with words I cannot find.

Inside, the phone rings.
"Where's Kate?" Dad asks.

I am here—but I say nothing.
He calls—but I do not answer.

"She's not in yet," he says to someone.
"I'll tell her you phoned."

I could go in.

Soon it will be suppertime anyway—
Time for eating and talking
    and being part of things,
Belonging again to the horrible, boring, nice,
    funny, noisy, busy, angry,
    loving world of people.

I'll go in when I have to.
In half an hour, I'll even like it.

Now . . .
Now I'll stay out here,
Hugging my separateness, my oneness.

I am alone. I am lonely.
I am growing into me.

Then I found the first of the answers.

Emily and I were downtown. I had to buy some Bristol board to make posters for the Spring Festival. Somehow I got stuck on the Publicity Committee. (I think actually I volunteered, to get out of singing in the choir.) I thought I could maybe write an ad for the paper and that would do it. Instead, I was stuck with *six* posters. I draw posters only a shade better than I sing.

I practically had to break Dave Nelson's non-painting arm, but I finally persuaded him to take over the poster-painting. His only condition was that I buy all the materials and deliver them to his front door. I don't know how he'd worked it, but he had managed not to be on any committee at all.

Our school tries to make this tremendous splash with a huge final concert in which every single student has some part. Every student but David Nelson!

I complained about this at some length as Emily and I walked along.

"You're just scared of running into Mrs. Nelson when you take the stuff to his house," Emily told me.

"Why should she worry me?" I said airily. "According to you, I'm a half-and-half person myself."

"I should have said a halfwit," Emily said.

Neither of us was meaning anything much. We were just talking to hear ourselves talk. It was like summer. We were both in sandals. Our feet were not warm exactly but we felt liberated. In no time, school would be over. Well, what's one little month!

I was so busy going on about Mrs. Nelson that I didn't spot them until we were right on top of them. We all halted together at the crosswalk and waited for the light to change.

This can't be true, I thought. It's a mistake, an optical illusion.

"Hello, Kate," Mrs. Rosenthal said in an extra-friendly voice.

I swallowed and jerked my head at her.

Sheila muttered a greeting too, as though there was a gun jammed against her back. I guess, in a sense, there was. Her mother was looking right at her and waiting.

But that isn't what got to me; I'd known she was Sheila's mother almost from the beginning. It was who they had with them. Right there, large as life, holding her mother's hand, was my goofy little kid! A Rosenthal, for crying out loud! She was waiting too, her eyes fixed on me. Big shining happy eyes!

*Blast*!

"Hi, Susannah," I said.

"Hi, Kate," she returned and blushed.

*Pretty as a rose*—that was Susannah, all right.

The light changed, we all trooped across the street and, thank goodness, turned to go in opposite directions. As we parted, though, I saw Sheila look at Susan—and Emily looked at me the same way. They minded—minded that Susannah and I had something going between us, on our own.

"Kate, what's *with* you and the Rosenthals anyway?" Emily asked sharply. I heard Sheila, behind me, say in the same hard voice "Come *on*, Susan!"

"Susannah's my friend, if that's what you mean," I told Emily—Emily who was still going to be my friend when we were old ladies in wheelchairs.

She made no comment.

I tried to put things back in perspective. I grinned at her. "You know perfectly well that Sheila Rosenthal scores below zero as far as I'm concerned. Aren't you the one who tried to persuade me there might be some merit hidden away within her? Well, it didn't work. I remain unpersuaded."

Still no comment.

"I've only met Mrs. Rosenthal once and we hardly even spoke to each other. She came into the store one day, that's all."

We were moving along the sidewalk as I

talked. Emily seemed to have developed a sudden intense interest in cement. I decided to leave well enough alone, to stop explaining. Then I knew I had to say it again, had to get it clear between us.

"I don't know what it is about Susannah," I stumbled over the words and was angry at myself. My voice sharpened. "I didn't know she was a Rosenthal. I still can't believe it. I wonder if she's a neighbor maybe—"

"She's not," Emily stated flatly. "Jean Sutherland told me the other day who she was."

I stared at the side of her face, which was all I could see. She did not look up.

"Why didn't you tell me?"

"I didn't know it mattered," Emily said.

She had known though. She hadn't said anything on purpose. It wasn't important. But it was. We'd never kept things from each other before.

Sometimes it's strange, liking people and being liked. Emily was still Emily. She mattered more to me than anybody, not counting Dad and Mother. Yet Susannah mattered too. It didn't make sense but it was a fact. Emily was going to have to learn to live with it. Sheila too, I suspected. Because I was important to Susannah too. That was also a fact.

I did not know what to say now. We kept walking, neither of us speaking.

Does Sheila ever call her Susannah? I wondered. I doubted it. You wouldn't ask a sister. I wouldn't have asked Marilyn, that was for sure.

I knew, though, that Sheila must love Susan. Anybody would. Yet how must it be to look like Sheila, washed-out and straggly, and have a small sister whose face was so bright with beauty and life, a sister pretty as a rose?

Say something, Emily. Say something!

She didn't. I couldn't. I turned in at the stationery store. She halted, looking confused as though she'd just wakened up.

"Bristol board," I said. "Remember?"

I didn't mean to sound like that. The words sliced out at her before I could stop them.

"I remember," Emily said slowly and came in with me.

It should have been over and done with. But as I bought the stuff and counted out the money, I still felt jolted.

I knew why too.

At that moment, I did not like Emily. Oh, that's not right. I loved her. But she had no business minding me caring about Susannah. Maybe I should have been pleased she was jealous or whatever. But I wasn't. I was sorry—and stubborn. If Emily and I were the kind of friends we were meant to be, there must be room for Susan Rosenthal too.

I see it clearly now and I can put it in words even. Then I just felt it. I was mad and sad and muddled up.

As we turned to come out, I looked right into

my friend's face. Her lips were tight, her eyes unhappy.

I hardly know Susannah, I thought in a panic. Why not forget about her? She's not worth a fight with Emily.

I think that then I still could have forgotten about her. Maybe. I also knew I wouldn't. Emily would come around.

"Will you go with me to the Nelsons'?" I asked.

"As your bodyguard?" Emily inquired.

She was laughing. I had been right. Already things were okay.

"That is a gross exaggeration—but yes!" I told her.

"Who really has you scared—Mrs. Nelson or David?" teased Emily.

"Both," I admitted, against my better judgment.

I wasn't worried about Emily getting jealous of how I felt about Dave though; she liked him as much, and as hopelessly, as I did.

Not that he didn't like us back. That's David Nelson's one outstanding flaw. He likes everybody impartially. No favorites. Not one.

It wasn't my day. Mrs. Nelson was in, but her son wasn't. We sighed, left the Bristol board for him, and went on home.

We did not speak of the Rosenthals again that afternoon.

We did not speak of them all week. I convinced myself everything was fine, the way it had always been, the way it would go right on being. I mean, we hadn't even had a quarrel. So what was there to worry about?

Not one thing.

Then, *wham*! In twenty-four hours, everything went wrong. Really wrong. And this time, I couldn't fix it.

# 11

# Little girl lost

Nothing had been said at home of Mrs. Rosenthal's visit to the store. I thought about it plenty but I certainly didn't refer to it.

Mother said, "Slim, what on earth's the matter with you? You're like a bear these days."

"Nothing," he growled.

He'd snap out of it, every so often, and quote at us or tease. Then he'd draw into himself again.

I wanted to tell Mother. Maybe she could have helped if she understood. But I wasn't sure I understood. And for all I knew, he'd told her the whole thing when I wasn't around. I went on waiting. Nothing happened.

Then came my appointment with the dentist.

If life is a bowl of cherries, there is also a handful of prunes in there. And some rhubarb. (That character sketch of Emily's should have said I hated coconut, parsnips and rhubarb.) Going to the dentist is like a bite of rhubarb. Ugh!

It wasn't as bad as I expected though. When I came out, I felt freed. One side of my face was still numb; I'd had two fillings. (That's what happens when you don't have one of those motherly mothers. I just knew Sheila had been brought up to be a fanatic toothbrusher.) His office is a couple of miles away from our place. I stood at the bus stop, thinking ahead to my evening.

I was looking forward to it. Emily was coming over right after supper. She had something to tell me, she had said, and a new poem to show me. I had one to read to her too. I'd come up with it that day in school. It was called "So I'm Proud!"

I had written it at Jackie Bernstein and her speech, at my father, at my mother, at Sheila and at myself. It made me laugh just remembering it. It made me feel better about everything too.

Our history teacher says,
"Be proud you're Canadians!"
My father says,
"You can be proud you're Jewish."
My mother says,
"Stand up straight, Kate!
Be proud you're tall."

What I want to know is
When did I have a chance to be
Spanish or Hindu or short?

That was telling them!

I saw the bus coming and I fished for and found my last bus ticket. The bus rumbled to a stop. I put one foot up on the step—and glanced over at the other door.

There was Susannah Rosenthal—and she was crying!

"Are you coming or going, young lady?" the bus driver asked me.

"I'm not coming," I stammered. "Could you wait—no, never mind."

I was back on the sidewalk and had my arms around Susan. She was Susan now, all of a sudden. Not a special dream of a joyous little girl but an actual miserable child, shaking with sobs.

"What is it? Susan, don't!" I begged.

The bus pulled away.

"Oh, Kate, KATE!" she gasped and flung her arms around my neck, bumping my ear with her violin case.

She had been to her music lesson and she was on her way home.

"I had this," she gulped out and showed me.

It was *The Middle Moffat*, a battered library copy.

"I didn't see our stop. I was so interested. Then, I knew I'd gone too far—and I didn't know how to get home. But I had to get off! And it'll soon be DARK!"

It wasn't anywhere near dark yet, but I sympathized. Inside her, the shadows of night towered.

"Well, we'll just catch the next bus and I'll take you home," I said sensibly.

Then I thought. I thought of two things. One, I had no money and only one bus ticket. Two, I didn't know where the Rosenthals lived. I turned to Susan for help. She had no money either. Her mother had given her exactly enough for her music lesson and her bus ticket, the one she'd already bought. They lived on Leigh Crescent. It was somewhere past our place. Another half mile maybe.

I suppose I should have marched up to somebody's house and asked to phone. I even thought of it but we were in a part of town without private homes. There was a shopping center behind us, office buildings down one side of the street, a cleaner's, two huge apartments (the kind you have to know somebody to get in), and a greenhouse across from us. Anyway I'm chicken about asking for things like that. Sometimes I can. Other times, like then, it seems easier to do almost anything else.

Susannah looked up at me trustingly. Then she saw my face get grim and lost her faith in me.

"What'll we *do*?" she wailed.

I made myself take it easy and smile at her.

"We'll walk home," I said.

I learned a lot on that walk. I learned how heavy a child's violin case can grow. I learned that Mrs. Rosenthal said Sheila was "going through a phase." (That is one expression April spares me. Marilyn broke her of it, I think. So there is something to be said for Marilyn.)

"Mother says everything will be okay when Sheila makes some friends here," Susannah continued to confide.

"I thought she was friends with Jackie Bernstein," I said.

Well, we had to talk about something. We had blocks and blocks yet to go. I didn't want Susannah noticing.

"She used to come over a lot," said Susannah, "but now they have a color TV themselves."

She wasn't being catty. She simply stated what was obvious.

"Oh," was all I could find to say.

I stopped prying but she went on anyway. I heard about Marcus next: She said he was a magnificent brother. (Susannah delights in long words.) She missed Marc, now he was away. So did Sheila.

"I'm the spitting image of him," Susan boasted.

Again, unexpectedly, I felt a pang for Sheila. It wasn't fair being sandwiched in between those two.

"Me and Marc both take after Daddy," added the small girl at my side.

It was true. I could see it right away, much as I fought not to. Susan had her mother's warmth, her mother's heart-catching smile, but she also had her father's aliveness, his eyes narrowing in laughter, his dark swiftness.

It looked a lot better on Susannah though.

I don't know what got her started off on being Jewish. I'm sure I didn't. Back then, what would I have said? Still, all at once, she was informing me how amazed she was that she and Isaac Mason were the only Jewish kids in her class.

"In Toronto there were lots," she said. "Gordon and Danny and Judy and . . . Rob and . . . Esther and Karen. More than that even."

"How can you tell who is and who isn't?" I asked, in spite of myself.

"Isaac comes to the synagogue," she said simply. "You know, Kate."

I nodded and shifted the violin case to my other hand.

"I have a best friend," she chattered on, off on a new tack. "Her name's Trudy Cavanaugh. She can skip to five hundred, Kate, without stopping once!"

Right then I understood how Sheila felt, and Emily too. I hated that Trudy. I could just see her, a horrible smug child with a fat face.

"But she's not Jewish," I said.

Susannah stared up at me.

"No. That hasn't anything to do with her skipping, Kate," she said. "She tap-dances and she's very, very smart. She can multiply and carry in her head."

"Can't you?" I asked, jealous for her.

"Sure, when I'm paying attention. My mind wanders. That's what the teacher wrote on my report card."

I laughed. I knew how it was. I had one of those minds myself. That's where Sheila bogs down in math really. She can't jump at the right answer inside her head. She gets it right in the end, but she has to work it out all the way. She's come second in math ever since she arrived—and third in English. Emily and I have that English teacher eating out of our hands.

"My, it's a long way, isn't it?" Susan said, sighing.

I wanted to pick her up and carry her. I took the book from her instead. Then I was inspired.

"Let's pretend something," I suggested.

"Hansel and Gretel," said Susan at once, her tired face brightening. "You be Hansel. Oh, Hansel, do you think there are wolves in this forest?"

I shivered with her. Then I remembered I was her big brother.

"No, no, Gretel. Don't be so silly," I said gruffly. "There haven't been wolves around here for years and years."

"But what's that noise?" quavered Gretel.

"A squirrel. Only a squirrel."

"You know, Kate," Gretel said kindly, "I don't

think they have squirrels where Hansel and Gretel lived. Why not say a deer?"

"But Gretel might be frightened of a deer," I said.

"Oh, no. I love deer!" Gretel assured me.

We wound our way deeper into the forest. We found the witch's house. I warned Gretel that we should not eat that house.

"But I'm so hungry, Hansel," she said.

And I could tell that she didn't have to pretend hunger. If only I had a chocolate bar or something.

"Okay," I said. "Take a little bit, somewhere where it won't show."

"I don't think Hansel would say 'okay'," Susannah said solemnly. She took her games seriously.

Then, at last, we reached my house—my apartment building, rather. We rent the ground floor, so it seems like our house. I didn't know the way to Leigh Crescent exactly. Dad would drive her home, I thought.

"Come on in," I said.

Susannah hesitated. I didn't really notice it at the time. Only afterwards, thinking back, I saw that her face grew uneasy.

"Is this *your* house, Kate?" she asked, a formal note in her voice.

"Yes." I opened the door and held it for her with my knee. "I'll get Dad to drive us over to your place."

"Maybe I'd better not—" Susan started.

Then I guess she realized she had to. She gave her head a quick little shake.

"Okay," she said and marched into the hall.

"Kate!" She turned back, looking for me, her face frightened.

"I'm right here," I told her.

And I held her hand the rest of the way.

# 12

# Fathers

My parents were in the living room. Mother started up when she saw me. Before she took in the child half hidden behind me, she burst into speech.

"Kate, a girl phoned—"

She stopped.

"Mother, Dad," I said, "this is Susannah—I mean Susan—Rosenthal."

Mother sank back down on her chair. There was the queerest silence. I was getting used to things being queer, but somehow I wasn't ready for this. I guess I was pretty tired, for one thing. I was tired for myself and I felt all Susannah's weariness in me too. I knew what she wanted.

Her mother. Not food or a place to sit down. Not anything there in our living room. She wanted her mother and nothing, no one else. Her mother who was the kind you could lean against and cry and cry. My mother is not like that. Susannah could tell. She made no attempt to go to April.

"Is Sam Rosenthal her father?" Dad asked.

It was like playing back a tape of my meeting with Dr. Rosenthal. Susan answered as I had, only without the coldness. She just sounded like an exhausted little girl.

"He's my daddy," she said.

I rushed in then with an explanation and Mother interrupted to say that must have been Susan's sister on the phone. They were looking for her.

"She sounded terribly upset," Mother said. "I don't know whatever made them think *you* might know where she was, Kate."

I couldn't explain it. Sheila had only seen Susan and me together that one time. We had hardly spoken: *Hi, Susannah. Hi, Kate.*

That had been all there was to it. Except we were friends and Sheila had remembered. She must have been clutching at straws.

"They expected her home a couple of hours ago. Do you realize it's almost seven o'clock?" Mother went on.

Susannah began to cry. She didn't make a sound. Tears simply spilled out of her eyes and down her cheeks.

"Come on," Dad said. "I'll take you home."

He came swiftly over to us, looked down at her, hesitated as she had done earlier, and then gathered her up in his arms the way I had wanted to.

He loves her, I thought. How could he not?

"It's all right, little one," he told her, right into her ear. "I'll take you to Elsa. This very minute."

"I'll call and tell them you're coming," Mother said.

(Later she explained she couldn't get the line. They were still phoning everyone Susan knew, trying to find her.)

I went too. I didn't ask permission or anything. I just followed along. In the car, I held Susan on my lap—violin case, book, and all.

Lights were on everywhere in the Rosenthals' house. I guess they'd searched the rooms, again and again, hoping somehow she was there and they'd missed her.

Dad took her from me and went ahead of me up the walk. I noticed she had both arms around his neck. She knew a friend when she met one, my Susannah.

The front door stood open. I reached out to ring the bell.

"Don't bother," Dad told me. "They need her now."

He hesitated, though, on the doorstep.

He was saved having to walk right in. Mrs. Rosenthal appeared right then, and saw us.

"Susan, oh, Susan!" she cried.

The next instant, she'd grabbed her. She went on crying, shaking Susan, hugging her, thanking Dad, asking us what had happened, not waiting for answers, hugging Susan again as though she planned to hold onto her forever and ever. Susannah hugged back and also joined in the crying. These, though, were tears of joy and relief.

Sheila stood and looked from Susan to me. She said not a word. I didn't say anything either. We were in the living room by now. I was watching our fathers. Dr. Rosenthal looked different. The hardness was gone. His face was marked with fear—and the same love I had seen on Dad's face when he first took Susannah up into his arms.

And something else. A kind of joyful anger. That doesn't make sense but that was how it seemed to me. As though he was mad at Dad, really mad— but glad he was there. Really glad too.

"Thank you, Nathan," he said.

My father cleared his throat, made a motion with his hands to say it was nothing, half turned to go back through the door we'd just entered, and then knew that wasn't enough, I guess. He turned back.

"Sam," he said, "I . . . what in God's name brought you to Riverside?"

"The job at the new clinic. It was what I wanted."

There was a tight silence. Except for Susannah, crying softly.

"I didn't want you here," my father said.

But it was as though he said the opposite. The words were full of something good, something warm.

"I'll bet you didn't," Dr. Rosenthal said. "I hadn't counted on turning up on your doorstep myself."

"You haven't changed much," my father said.

"Well, you have. I guess I have, too. It's been twenty-six years."

My father said, "I know."

I was listening harder than I'd ever listened to anything. Sheila's ears were practically falling off, they were so busy taking it in. She *didn't* know the answers. At least, not all of them.

They're friends, I thought.

Then it came to me. Of course; Sam . . . Sammy and . . . Phil. They were in Dad's stories too. They were brothers. Philip was older and the leader. Dad and Sammy were his to command. Abby used to get to play too by threatening to tell their father if Dad didn't let her.

Dr. Rosenthal was Sammy! It didn't seem possible. Yet it explained so much.

Had Mrs. Rosenthal been around too? I couldn't remember hearing of an Elsa.

"Abby . . . she's all right?" my father asked then.

Everything changed in that quarter of a second.

"I'll take care of Abby," Dr. Rosenthal said. He sounded like the one I'd met before. The hardness was back. "Phil left enough."

Dad straightened. His face stiffened too. I didn't know there had been a light in it till the light went out. He turned this time with purpose.

"Come on, Kate," he said to me.

"Sam!" Mrs. Rosenthal cried.

"Good-bye, Nathan," Dr. Rosenthal said.

"Aren't you even going to shake hands, after all this time?" Mrs. Rosenthal left Susan and hurried over to stand between us and her husband.

My father looked back. He smiled at her.

"You have a lovely little girl there, Elsa," he said. "Try to keep track of her. Come, Kate."

We started down the walk. Sheila's mother pushed open the screen door and called after us.

"Nathan! Nathan, I'd like to meet your wife!"

"We're in the phone book," my father said. "Stay well, Elsa."

We got into the car. We didn't speak for a couple of blocks. Then I couldn't stand it.

"He's the Sammy you knew when you were little, isn't he?" I asked, afraid to, but bound and bent to know.

"Yes, he's that Sammy. And his brother Philip was married to your Aunt Abigail. He died a couple of years ago. And I don't want to discuss it further, Katharine—"

"When did you last see Aunt Abby?" I burst out.

I thought he wasn't going to answer. Then he said slowly and wearily, "Twenty-six years ago."

I did not say another word.

# 13

# Wall

If Mother had only remembered to tell me that Emily came that night while I was gone! Afterwards, when I asked her about it, trying to shift the blame, she said Emily had told her it wasn't important. That must have been right after my mother said, "She's over at Sheila Rosenthal's." That was the truth, after all. How was April to know her choice of words mattered?

I don't really blame Mother for forgetting anyway. When I came back from the Rosenthals', Dad came too. If it's a choice between me and my father, I never have to wonder who'll come first with Mother. Marilyn used to gripe about it but I don't mind. He comes first with me too.

Anyway, I myself knew Emily was planning to come over. I should have remembered to call her. Only it was after eight when we got back and I hadn't had any supper yet. By the time I'd finished and cleaned up the kitchen it was nearly nine. I had a stack of homework waiting.

I just forgot Emily entirely. All I could think about was what had happened at Susannah's, what Mrs. Rosenthal had said, the way they all looked, the weariness in my father's voice when he said "Twenty-six years ago."

In bed, I did think, Oh, I should have called Emily, but that was because I wanted to tell her about Susannah being lost. I still didn't remember our plans.

I guess the whole business had me worn out. I don't think I thought another thought. I plunged straight into sleep.

Emily and I met at school the next morning. She'd had to go early for choir practice. I was wondering how much I should tell her about the Rosenthals. Some of it was Dad's business.

So, in the beginning, it *was* my fault. That much I can see now. Then the whole thing hit me like a thunderbolt and I did all the wrong things.

"So?" Emily said frostily, before I could get my mouth open.

"So what?" I answered blankly.

She blinked. She'd expected an instant apology, I guess.

"So where were you?" she asked.

She was giving me a chance to explain. She was also taking great pains to act as though it didn't really matter. I remained as dense as a brick wall. It was incredible.

"Where was I when?" I said.

"Last night. Remember me, Kate? I'm the friend you asked over but when I got there, your mother said you'd gone out."

The light dawned.

"Oh, yeah. Sure!" I said. But I was still only half with it. I blundered on. "I was over at Sheila's."

Mother's not the only one who can put her foot squarely between her teeth.

Emily's face closed like a bank vault. There I was, repentant at last. She was not interested. I must say Emily doesn't come out of this blamelessly either. She *could* have listened.

"Oh," she said. Brushing my beginning of an explanation aside, she continued coldly, "I just didn't realize you'd really taken up with Sheila, that's all. I mean, when you said you didn't like her, I believed you. My mistake!"

I did not like Sheila Rosenthal. So why didn't I simply say so and get that fact straight between us once and for all? I don't know why. It suddenly seemed *my* business, not Emily's. What if I had taken up with Sheila? I hadn't—but suppose I had? It shouldn't have made any difference between Emily and me. I

got a bit cold myself. I ignored all reference to
Sheila and let go my chance to fix things.

"What did you have to tell me anyway?" I
asked. I hurried because the bell was about to
ring.

Emily reddened. She shifted her stack of
books around a bit. She did not look at me.

If she'd just looked at me then, straight on,
the way she always had. But she didn't.

"I guess you wouldn't be interested," she said,
half angrily, half battling her own uncertainty,
"I'm—I'm becoming a member of the church at
a special service next Friday night. I was just
going to invite you to come, that's all."

She had been attending classes to learn
about it for ages. I knew it was coming. She'd
even talked before about asking me. She was
getting a new dress, more grown up than any
she'd had before. I'd planned to go and she
knew that.

How, though, do you accept an invitation
which isn't being offered any longer? I didn't
know how. I said the first words I could find.
Stupid, wrong words!

"I guess I wouldn't belong there," I said. "I'm
going to be busy anyway."

If I'd wanted to knock Emily speechless, I had
my wish. She just stood. Then the bell rang. If it
hadn't, we might have backed down, even then,
and saved the situation.

We went on into our first class without

another word to each other. An awfulness went with us. We weren't ourselves at all—and neither of us knew what to do about it. I didn't hear much of the lesson although I do remember automatically answering a question—and surprising myself when I got it right. All the time I sat there, though, I was hating Emily. I couldn't stop. It hurt worse than anything I'd ever known before.

Things straightened out soon enough on the surface. Lindsay Ross helped. The three of us walked out of that class together and she said, all at once, "Hey, what's wrong with you two? Have you had a fight?" She thought she was kidding.

"No," I snapped too loudly.

And Emily, at the same instant, told her, "Of course not."

So, after that, we had to talk. I think I said something about liking her new sweater. No, that must have been another time. But that was the way we began. Saying meaningless things. I think we both believed that, any minute now, it would be okay down underneath too.

It wasn't.

I didn't show her the poem "So I'm Proud!" It was about being different, sort of. I did show her another one I'd written, one about school. It was called "Today."

Today I will not live up to my potential.
Today I will not relate well to my peer group.
Today I will not contribute in class—
    I will not volunteer one thing.
Today I will not strive to do better.
Today I will not achieve or adjust
    or get involved or grow enriched.
I will not put up my hand even if
    the teacher is wrong and I can prove it.
Today I might eat the eraser off my pencil.
I'll look at clouds.
I'll be late.
I don't think I'll wash.
I need a rest!

Emily laughed with me, almost the way Emily always had. She understood it completely, of course. We were enriched up to our ears those days.

But under our laughter, there was still a wall. A wall we did not know how to break through. A wall each of us blamed the other for building. A wall which would get higher and more frightening in the days ahead.

Why didn't she say "Kate, I'm sorry. Come to the service."

Why didn't I say "Emily, I didn't mean what I said. You know I want to come."

I suppose I was waiting for her to go first. She was waiting too.

# 14

# The different summer

I think we'd still have managed to right things if school hadn't ended. Emily left for a trip out west with her parents and Louisa.

My parents thought her parents were crazy. The Blairs said they'd always wanted to see the Rockies and they believed in traveling while you were still young. Louisa was that, all right.

Mother wanted to send me to camp again, but I finally persuaded her not to. Camp is great— for some kids. Some camps. The one they'd shipped me off to the last couple of years was a fakey outfit. They went in for all sorts of Indian rituals no real Indian would be caught dead at. The kids were there mostly because their parents didn't know what else to do with them.

To be honest, that was why mine had sent me. Before I met Emily, I used to be a brat. It was complicated, and I'm not going back over it now. My parents had decided that I needed supervision—and they were not child supervisors. Since then, I've grown up some (no thanks to the camp).

Lots of the kids at camp were case histories and they reveled in it. That bugged me. I don't like listening to girls swapping stories about how their mothers and fathers got divorced. They'd brag about how they could play their parents off one against the other.

There were quite a few mixed-marriage kids there too, ones whose mothers and fathers hadn't made it. It gave me the creeps. I knew that nothing could ever take my mother and my father away from each other—nothing short of death. But at that dumb camp, I'd get to wondering.

I didn't tell Mother any of that, of course. She'd have hit the roof. Or maybe laughed—you never can be sure with April. I just told her about the phony Indian stuff. Mother likes everything authentic—no fooling around—so the Indian line worked.

"But what will you do if you don't go to camp?" she asked me.

"I want to read," I said. "And be lazy. And maybe I'll do some baby-sitting and earn a fortune."

That's just about what I did, too. It was a different summer, one I'll always remember. I began to read books at random, but soon I was reading everything I could find about being Jewish. My parents must have noticed it. I mean, the books were all over the place. But they didn't say anything.

I read *Heaven Help Us* and *The Chosen* and *Berries Goodman* and *The Diary of Anne Frank* and *The Endless Steppe* and *The City Boy* and *Portrait of Deborah*, and others too.

One thing about the books fascinated me. When they were really good, I forgot why I was reading them. I don't know how to explain that. But some of them were so busy preaching about prejudice that I felt outside them. Yet I *was* the girl in *The Endless Steppe*, and I cried over Anne Frank, and I laughed and laughed at that crazy Herbie Bookbinder in *The City Boy*.

I read history, even. I'd never liked history except when it came in a story about a lonely queen or a brave explorer or something dramatic. Jewish history, though, seemed fascinating. One author said that six Jews had changed the world's history and he listed them—Jesus, Paul, Karl Marx, Albert Einstein, Sigmund Freud, and a philosopher called Spinoza. I'd never heard of Spinoza (though I've heard Dad talk about him since). I began to see that Jackie Bernstein wouldn't have had much trouble finding stuff to base her speech on.

I read about Jewish holidays, how they began and how they are celebrated today. I tried to feel inside me what they must mean to people who are Jewish. Dad probably knew when those days came. And he had never said anything.

I read about Hillel. I read part of a book by Martin Buber, and I couldn't understand a word of it. I read about Maimonides and wondered how to pronounce his name. I wanted to ask Dad, but I didn't.

One day, though, I asked him if he'd take me to the synagogue. His face darkened. Then I could see him making himself relax.

"Yes, Kate, I'll take you," he said. "But not here. I'll take you to Toronto. As soon as I'm free."

"Why not here?" I said. "Sheila goes here."

Reading about Jews and how they stuck to their ways and their faith through thick and thin must have made me braver.

Dad muttered something about the rabbi in Riverside being a fossil.

"You mean he's Orthodox?" I asked.

I tried to sound offhand about it, as though I knew exactly what I was talking about—even if it did all come from books.

Dad saluted my casualness with a quick grin.

"No," he said, "as a matter of fact, the congregation is Conservative—but he wishes they were Orthodox. I promise I will take you sometime, Kate, and we'll talk about it then."

Maybe he forgot. I doubt it. He never offered to take me. Anyway, things were awfully busy at the store. We keep open Friday nights. And Saturday. So I didn't say anything more.

By the time summer was nearly over, I'd begun to change. I'd always been afraid of God; I'd kept out of His way, and counted on Him leaving me alone. When Emily had tried to talk to me about Him, I'd dodged. I knew she believed in the things her church taught her, but I thought I didn't believe in anything. Who needed it? I thought I'd shut my ears to the whole works—and stay free.

God was beginning to get to me now, though. I guess maybe I was letting Him.

I waited and waited for a letter from Emily. Finally a postcard came. She hadn't exactly rushed. It came all the way from Vancouver.

> Dear Kate,
> The mountains are beautiful. Mother says the prairies are too but I got bored. Louisa is being angelic.
>
> > See you,
> > Emily

Not "love," I noticed, trying not to. I was glad I didn't have an address to write back to, because I had nothing to say. I hadn't seen or heard from the Rosenthals all summer. That was the one thing I wanted to tell Emily. But I couldn't have written it down. Besides, it shouldn't have mattered.

That much I was right about. But I was letting it matter as much as Emily did.

In August, the week before she was due back, I started to read the Bible. All I'd known before were Scripture readings in school, which I mostly didn't listen to, and bits Dad quoted.

I read an old copy of Mother's which I found on a bookshelf in our hall. It had terribly small print, but I stuck with it.

I read it in secret. That was really funny. I felt as though I was reading a dirty book that my parents would have a fit about me having. (Not that my parents have ever kept me from reading anything, but still.) I would shut the door to my room at night and get into bed and read it. And I kept the covers ready to shove it under and another book handy to pretend I'd been reading if they came in. They didn't ever come.

Lots of it was awful. Other parts I didn't understand. I couldn't believe my eyes when I found that story about Elisha and the bears. Then I got going on the story of David's life one night and I couldn't quit. I've never heard anybody say he couldn't put the Bible down, but that was about it.

I got as far as Proverbs—and then school began and I bogged down. I am going to go on, but I think I'll skip the rest of Proverbs. It was dull.

When I began thinking back over things, I promised myself that I wouldn't lie, and I just did. The real reason I bogged down in Proverbs is that I came on a part that hurt too much, that's all. It was late at night and I was tired already. Suddenly, I came to a part about friendship.

Faithful are the wounds of a friend;
but the kisses of an enemy are deceitful.
The full soul loatheth an honeycomb;

but to the hungry soul every bitter thing
is sweet.

As a bird that wandereth from her nest,
so is a man that wandereth from his place.

Ointment and perfume rejoice the heart;
so doth the sweetness of a man's friend . . .

If I'd read that six months before, it wouldn't
have meant a thing to me. But now each word
made sense. Especially that bit about the bird
wandering from her nest.

I cried. And that's why I quit reading Proverbs.

We went back to school. We were in high
school now. It was huge and bewildering at first.
Emily and I were put in different classes, different homerooms. We couldn't even share a locker;
you had to share with somebody in your homeroom. (Sheila was in my homeroom but we did
not share a locker.)

I was almost too busy to miss Emily.

No. That is a lie too.

I missed her all the time.

But we hadn't time to say more than Hi when
we passed each other in the hall. We could have
made the time to say more. It would have been
very simple. I wanted to. I thought about it. But
I waited for Emily to make the first move.

It wasn't simple at all.

# 15

# Mothers

Emily and I lost touch.

I've heard people say that. They say it lightly. "Then I lost touch with her," they say calmly. It wasn't a light thing for Emily and me.

The days did keep passing though. Ever since I was very small, whenever something seemed too much to bear and I'd spill it out to Mother, she'd look at me and say, "The sun will rise tomorrow, Kate, just the same." I used to hate her saying that. But it's true. And, in a queer way, it's comforting. Something is sure.

I started going to the store after school regularly then. I'd gone before in the spring, but not directly from school. Emily and I used to loiter and talk and I'd arrive at BLOOMFIELD'S BOOKS around five. If I skipped going, nobody said anything. But now I went the minute school let out. I still wasn't old enough to be hired officially. I did it because I wanted to, not for pay. In between finding books for people, I read and read and read.

Of course, it meant Emily and I did not walk home together any longer. I told myself I was glad. It would have been awkward. I tried not to wonder if she'd found somebody else to walk with instead.

She was busier herself. She had explained this to me just as I'd told her at length about how much they needed me at the store. Louisa was a handful-and-a-half, now that she'd started walking, and Mrs. Blair welcomed Emily with cries of joy when she arrived to take over "that child."

"That's what they call her now all the time," Emily said, laughing. "That child!"

I laughed too. (But I missed that child almost as much as I missed Emily.)

Twice I baby-sat the Sutherland kids when Emily couldn't, but something was wrong there too, a different something.

Emily's Aunt Deborah doesn't like me much. Lindsay's mother is the same. They both think I'm a bad influence. (I guess maybe I was, a bit, when I first knew Lin.) But I think really they don't like my being Jewish. I just think that; they've never said. I have a feeling they don't say it even to themselves. It's something they feel without thinking. Maybe that's partly what prejudice is—feeling without thinking.

Anyway, when Emily offered to arrange for me to baby-sit a third time, I said I was busy. That ended that.

Then, one day late in September, I met Mrs. Blair on the street. I pretended I didn't see her, but she wouldn't have it. She stepped over in front of me so I had to stop.

"Kate," she said, "what is it? What's happened between you and Emily? We haven't seen you for weeks."

"Nothing," I stammered.

She went on looking at me. Her eyes are so like Emily's. Everything about her is like Emily. She even has long hair.

"I hope you work it out soon," she told me. "We all miss you, Kate. Louisa especially."

"Well, there's a lot to do at the store," I mumbled.

"I met your mother the other day," she answered. "I asked her about that. She says it's much as usual . . . all right, I won't pry any further. But do work it out. Emily needs you."

Mrs. Blair had put her hand on my arm. Now she let me go. I hesitated, searching for words. But there was nothing. I almost ran away from her.

I slowed down, at the end of the block. Then the words were there in a flood.

Why me? Why can't Emily work it out? If she needs me so much, I'm right here.

At that, Dad's voice sounded, like a harsh echo, in my memory.

*She knows where to find me*, he had said.

Was this how he felt? Had something like this happened between him and his sister? I still didn't know, but his sadness was inside me now. I understood it too well.

I'm making those days sound completely bad and sad, though. They weren't. Right about then, I read *The Lord of the Rings*. I'd never liked books about elves and stuff but Hobbits are something else. I went around for weeks feeling that people were too big.

Mother joined the bridge club about then too.

"April, don't do it," Dad warned her. "You haven't a mathematical mind."

"I'm as mathematical as Elizabeth Blair," Mother said. "Besides, they don't go just for bridge, they say. They go for conversation."

Dad looked dubious but she went anyway. Twice. Then she told them, and us, that she was quitting.

"But why?" Dad asked, as he had done about her weaving. Mother looked sheepish and defiant at one and the same time.

"I'm plenty mathematical enough," she maintained. Then she confessed, "I keep falling asleep."

Dad roared. She glared at him.

"I'll have you know I won a prize, asleep or awake," she said.

It turned out she'd brought home the Booby Prize but she didn't admit that till she'd made him apologize. The two of them laughed like idiots.

I thought it was funny too, but also kind of sad. I knew how Emily's mother enjoyed that bridge club. Mother was just plain tired and, working in the store all the time, she wasn't in on the things the others talked about. I felt sorry for her. I don't think she felt sorry for herself. Self-pity is one of the things she's against.

Then Mrs. Rosenthal came to our house.

It took her awhile. Months had passed since that night she had called after Dad, "Nathan, I want to meet your wife." Maybe she hoped the two men would get things straightened out on their own if she left them to it long enough. I guess she was afraid too. Kids aren't the only shy people in the world.

But one golden afternoon early in October I came in—and there she was. She looked like a visitor. She had on gloves even. And she looked nervous.

Mother looked just as nervous, only Mrs. Rosenthal would have no way of knowing that. Mother gets brittle and talks too much and is extra gay when she's scared. She was chattering at such a pace I wanted to pull on the reins and say "Whoa—steady!" I gave moral support instead.

Mrs. Rosenthal was telling Mother about my aunt. I listened to some of it. She was very lonely, Mrs. Rosenthal said. She said Aunt Abby had a fine boy, but that was not enough. She said my aunt was only fifty.

*Only,* I thought, but I didn't say anything.

She left before Dad came in. Mother turned into her real self just at the end.

"Thank you, Elsa, for coming," she said. "I mean it."

"I should have come before," Mrs. Rosenthal answered, "but I didn't know what you'd be like."

They stood there, looking at each other. And all at once, I saw they weren't so different. No more different than Emily and I were.

Oh, Emily . . .

I left Mother to see Mrs. Rosenthal out, and went to start supper.

"Kate has become domesticated," Mother told Dad that night.

I'd made tea biscuits. I'd pounded them into shape, letting loose all my pent-up feelings on the dough. It wasn't the way the home economics teacher had told us to do it but it seemed necessary at the time. Dad chewed hard on what was supposed to be a flaky, tender mouthful.

"Tamed, maybe," he commented. "Domesticated, not quite.

# 16

# My family

Sometime when I wasn't around, Mother must have told Dad all about Sheila's mother's visit. Somehow, she was able to make him listen to reason. I don't know how, because I think Mother has been shut out by that closed door too. Anyway, after all those years, my father went to see his father.

And I went with him, to meet my grandfather.

Dad didn't intend to take me. I don't think he was even going to tell me anything about it. But Mother wakened with a migraine headache that Sunday morning. She doesn't have them often but when she does, we leave her alone. That is the one thing she wants, to be left alone.

Dad went into the darkened room where she was lying.

"All right," he said. "I'm taking her with me. But you didn't need to go to these lengths, April."

Mother laughed. It sounded more like a groan.

"Good," she said. "I've said, from the beginning—"

"I know," Dad broke in. "I've heard you."

Then Mother said the astonishing thing.

"God go with you, Jonathan," she told him.

Dad did not say a word that I could hear. Maybe he kissed her. Maybe he ignored her. I don't know. But we were on our way to Toronto ten minutes later.

He told me some of the answers as we drove, although I could tell he didn't really want to talk. Most of it I'd guessed by that time, but he filled in gaps.

The break with his family had come, not when he left home, but when he came back again to tell his father that he wanted to marry April Whittaker.

I suppose I should have guessed that too but I hadn't. They were both very young.

"We were practically in the cradle," Dad said.

Mother's parents were already elderly then. They both died not long afterward. They were not too concerned when she told them she was getting married to a Jew.

"Her mother wasn't 'well enough' to come to the wedding though," Dad quoted dryly. "If you'd call it a wedding. It was a civil ceremony."

I'd known that.

"My father forbade me to marry her," Dad said.

He looked straight ahead at the road. I glanced at his profile. Then I looked at the road too.

"He said, if I did, I was never to come home again. He refused to see her. I begged him to meet her, just once. Although what good that would have done, I don't know. Even April couldn't have changed his whole way of thinking in one meeting. But I did marry her, Kate, and we've been happy. I was angry, terribly angry. I rejected everything he had ever taught me. I threw away what my mother had taught me too. Now that I'm older, I know more of what he went through." He paused, drew breath, went on.

"Abby stood by us as long as she dared. She . . . well, she couldn't stand up to him openly. At first, I got little letters from her—but they soon stopped. I did know she married Phil. Sam and I were close friends and Philip and I were nearly as close. Yet Sam could not understand my turning against all that we'd been taught was important. He wouldn't meet April either. None of them ever really cared. They just knew she wasn't Jewish. That made her . . . I can't explain, Kate."

"It's okay," I said. "I know."

What'll I marry? I thought suddenly, painfully.

An instant later, I changed that.

Not what. Who. I'll marry a person. Not a Jew, not a gentile. A person.

And yet, this person . . . he'd have to be something.

I thought of Dave Nelson. I wondered briefly what Dad would say about me marrying a boy who was part native and whose mother insisted there was no God.

Suddenly, words I'd learned from the Bible came to me.

He that walketh uprightly, and wor-
keth righteousness and speaketh the
truth in his heart. . .

It was the part about speaking the truth in his heart I'd especially liked. That, I told myself, was what I would look for. I laughed inside, picturing myself asking my countless suitors whether or not they walked uprightly. I did not share my thoughts with Dad. They weren't shareable thoughts.

"Sam still keeps a kosher house—or sees that Elsa does," Dad went on, talking to himself. "I don't know whether we could communicate about what's at the center of it all or not. Sam isn't much for looking at the center."

Was this what Dr. Rosenthal had meant about Dad thinking himself a cut above the rest of the world or whatever it was he'd said?

The car stopped. The house was narrow and

brown with a tiny square of lawn in front. The windows looked at us blankly.

"Come on," he said.

He sounded like a stranger. I followed him up to the door. He reached for the knob, hesitated, reddened a little and rang the bell. My Aunt Abigail answered the door.

For less than an instant, her eyes rested on Dad's face without recognition. Then, before he had to speak, she knew him.

"Nathan," she whispered.

She stood there, not moving, staring at him. I've heard of people looking as though they were seeing a ghost. She looked exactly like that.

My father smiled at her. Oh, it was a smile such as I've never seen—except, once in a while, he does look that way at Mother, when she's asleep.

"I'm coming in, Abby," he said gently. "So let me. This is my Kate."

She was frightened then. Her hands twisted together. She still barred the way in.

"My son, he's out there . . . around the side of the house," she gabbled. "Wouldn't she . . . couldn't she go and play with him?"

I drew back.

How big was this kid? I didn't "play" much any more.

Except with Susannah, I remembered.

Dad turned from her to me.

"Go find him, Kate," he said. "I'll call you when I want you."

I walked away from the two of them, my back very stiff.

Twice he had called me Kate. Yet he almost always called me Katharine. I battled tears but I would not have gone back for anything. I had been sent away like a child. Like a child, I hugged my hurt.

Then I found Sol, raking up the last of the leaves.

He was old enough to shave, for crying out loud! Much, much too grown up to play games with. I stopped near him and just stood, not knowing what to do or say. He put down his rake.

"And who might you be?" he asked, looking friendly.

He was like Dr. Rosenthal with a dash of Dad thrown in. It was eerie. I quit wanting to cry. I was in the middle of a drama, all at once, and searching for the perfect next line.

"I am Katharine Bloomfield, your cousin."

"Oh, are you! Well, in that case, I am Sol Rosenthal, *your* cousin," he returned, laughing at me.

Neither of us even pretended we weren't staring. It was much too interesting.

"Saul—like King Saul?" I asked, impressed.

"No. Sol—like King Solomon," he corrected. "Solomon Enoch Rosenthal, if you must know."

I hunted through my memory. There was something there, some tag end left from my Bible reading . . .

"Enoch . . . walked with God?" I tried.

"That's the one," Sol said. He looked slightly startled though. I knew how he felt. Outwardly I remained calm.

"I thought you were an infidel," he said then, lightly.

He was asking me a question, I knew, but I did not know the answer. I dodged. I was used to dodging that particular question by now.

"You'd be surprised what we infidels know," I tossed back.

I was hoping that Dad would hurry. This conversation was too much. I'd never be able to keep it up.

I think Sol guessed. He took pity on me anyway.

"Is your father in the house?" he said.

I nodded.

"Why didn't he take you in with him?"

I stalled, not wanting to explain the scene at the door. Again he guessed.

"Mother chickened out and wouldn't let you in, I'll bet," he said. "She probably thinks you'd be bad for Grandfather's blood pressure. I don't suppose you'd do it any good, at that."

He didn't seem to expect an answer.

"So my Uncle Jonathan is in there . . . I've always wanted to see what he looks like, since I found out about him. I used to think he was dead."

This time, I took pity. "Well, I've wanted to see your grandfather, ever since I discovered he existed."

For an instant I was afraid I'd made things worse instead of better, but he looked relieved.

"Our grandfather," he corrected me. "Oh, he exists, all right," he added with a wry twist to his mouth. "He's quite something, in fact. You know, you ought to be in there. You should see him. We're acting like people in the Middle Ages! Did your father say you weren't to come in?"

I shook my head.

"Mother's been scared of Grandfather all her life," Sol said matter-of-factly. "It would probably do him good to get shaken up a bit. Come on. I'll take you in."

We started around the house.

"It can't hurt anything," he muttered as we went. I knew then that Aunt Abigail wasn't the only one who was afraid of this grandfather of ours.

Not only was Sol more scared than he would admit, he was wrong about my going in not hurting anything. But I didn't know that. I wanted to go myself. I can't put the blame on Sol.

When we got to the back door, we had both stopped pretending to be brave. He eased it open as cautiously as though he were out to filch the family silver. He pointed for me to go first. I hung back but he looked impatient.

Coward! I jeered at myself—and I tiptoed ahead of him.

The minute I put my foot over the doorsill, I

wanted to turn and run. But Sol was right behind me, blocking the way back. Standing close together there in the dark kitchen, we could feel each other's tension.

"Hey, listen," he whispered, about six inches from my ear. "Let's just look at them and scram. I know where we can see in without them noticing us."

"Okay," I whispered back.

"Be *quiet*!" he ordered, also in a whisper.

His whisper sounded deafening to me. I scowled at him.

"I am." I mouthed the words at him this time.

He grinned at that, seeing how silly he was being. But it was a shadowy grin and it only lasted a second.

We crept out of the kitchen and down the hall. At the foot of a narrow flight of stairs stood an open door. Through it came voices.

One more step . . . another . . . another.

I halted. Sol bumped into me and stopped too. We could both see into the room.

There he was—my grandfather!

He didn't look the way I had imagined he would. I thought of him as being the way I picture Moses, with fierce eyes and a huge white beard and hands raised over people to denounce them or instruct them, I'm not sure which. Grandfather's eyes could be fierce enough but at that moment, they were just tired. He actually did have a beard but it was wispy and sort of streaked. He was almost bald. His suit was creased and worn at the knees as though he had had it on for days. He did have one hand lifted a little but not commandingly. From where I stood, I could see it shaking.

He was saying something in a thin high voice, almost the voice of a child. I listened.

". . . great-grandson. What's his name?"

Dad was telling him about Nicky, I thought in astonishment—Marilyn's little boy. And Grandfather was listening! At that moment, Dad moved a step closer to the old man. Light shone in through a window on my father's face. I wanted to run to him but I didn't move. I felt braver, though, just seeing him there.

"So that is my Uncle Jonathan," Sol whispered.

I turned my head slightly.

"Does he look the way you thought he would?" I breathed.

"I thought he'd be taller and thinner. How about Grandfather?"

"I thought he'd look like Moses," I told my cousin.

"Who says he doesn't?" Sol said. He was speaking so softly I barely caught the words. "Come on. Let's beat it."

I inched backwards but there was a loose board. *Creak*!

"Who is out there?"

My grandfather's voice sounded out strong and sure all at once. I knew we hadn't a chance.

"Sorry," I muttered at Sol.

He patted my back.

"Not your fault," he said. "Stand up to him no matter what. That's what he likes."

"I said who—is—out—there? Solomon! Come here to me."

The two of us marched into the room, side by side. I could feel my knees literally knocking. I kept my head up, though, and I made myself look straight at him. Yes, his eyes were every bit as fierce as the eyes of Moses when he spotted the golden calf.

Dad spoke first.

"This is my younger daughter, Katharine," he said.

I darted a glance at him. He smiled. The smile didn't quite make it to his eyes but I knew he did not mind me being there.

Not yet.

It was Grandfather who said it. Suddenly, catching me off guard, he came out with the thing that so startled me that I wrecked everything.

"The child looks like Bess," he said.

I love Bess. I do. I always have and I always will. Still, I knew who I looked like. I'd been hearing it my whole life. I didn't stop to think. The words just came.

"I do not," I said. "I look like Mother."

# 17

# Afterwards

What happened next happened all at once and in a matter of seconds. Yet I will remember each part of it separately as long as I live.

My aunt put both hands up over her mouth and made a little choking noise. I think, if she could have, she would have run. She looked incredibly small. She isn't quite as tall as I am. (My height is one of the things I get from my mother. )

Sol took three giant steps and was at her side. He deserted me without a backward glance or a steadying word. I was glad when he did it. He was where he should be. I was not frightened.

Awed, yes. Uncertain about what I had done or what I should do next. But still not frightened.

My father . . . I did not understand what he did. Not then. Now I do. Now I know that he did not hear what I said to Grandfather. He heard only what his father had said first. He stared at me as though he had never seen me before. Stared and stared. Then his face lighted from within.

He was not looking at *me* that way. He was looking at his mother.

"It's true," he said. "And I have never seen it. Not once. Your eyes . . . I only saw April. Bess's hair was so black . . . but your eyes and—"

He stopped with that because Grandfather interrupted him.

If he had been old before, my grandfather, he was much older now. When I spoke so abruptly, his eyes flashed instant anger. But, almost immediately, the fire dimmed and snuffed out. He seemed to shrink, all at once. His clothes looked too big. His glance shifted away from me, from everyone. His voice, when it came, wavered shrilly. It was utterly unlike the voice that had summoned us into the room. He was not even remotely like Moses.

"Abigail, I want my supper," he said. "I want to be left alone."

It was as though we had already gone, although we both were standing right in front of him, my father and I. Dad tried to reach him once more.

"Father," he began.

He put out his hand, to touch his father's bent trembling fingers, and then waited instead. Grandfather did not seem to see that hand outstretched. Neither did he answer. He spoke again to my aunt, still in the high, cracked voice of a very, very old man.

"I need to rest, Abigail," he said. "You know I need to rest."

Then, suddenly, he fell asleep. I didn't know what had happened. His head dropped forward and his hands slid together between his knees. I started back, frightened at last, feeling responsible for whatever had happened.

Aunt Abigail ignored me. She never did speak to me directly. She appealed to Dad across the room.

"Nathan, you must go. You must."

Sol came back to me as quickly as he had gone.

"Come on," he ordered. "We can wait outside."

I stumbled after him in a daze. What was wrong with Grandfather? Did I really look like Bess?

Sol explained away my fear at once when we reached the front sidewalk. I think my face must have been white. I know I felt I might be sick.

"He's just asleep," he said. "It's okay. Don't look like that. He gets tired fast that way lots of times. Especially late in the day. He's over eighty, you know."

He seemed five hundred to me.

"I didn't mean—" I started unhappily. "It's just that I've always been told I look like Mother. I do too. I know I do."

"You also look like Grandmother," Sol told me. "I've seen her picture when she was young. Your father's right. It's your eyes—and from what I've heard about her, your nerve too."

"That could be Mother," I said.

"Katharine!"

I turned instantly. We had moved away from the front door, out of harm's way. I ran back. There was urgency in my father's voice, as though he were afraid he'd lost me.

"Here I am," I called.

He looked relieved, but tired too. Terribly, terribly tired.

"Hello, Sol," he said to the tall boy behind me. "I hear you're off to college next year."

"Yes, sir," Sol said, standing very straight.

"Your mother has my address. I'll help any way I can. I'm sorry I haven't . . . well, I'll help when you need me," Dad said.

Sol looked at him. I was afraid then. I waited for rejection to cloud his face. He grinned suddenly, sweetly—like Susannah Rosenthal.

"Thanks, Uncle Nathan," he said.

"It'll be my pleasure," Dad told him.

He sounded as though he had a cold.

My aunt did not come out. I guess her father needed her. Maybe she didn't want to see me again—but I don't really believe that. She's not the strongest person in the world, Aunt Abby. It had been quite an afternoon.

I'll bet she was crying somewhere.

Dad and I rode along, not speaking for the first twenty or thirty miles. Finally he broke the silence.

"Well, Elsa should be satisfied, at least," he said. "I did try. But it wasn't going well, even before you arrived on the scene. It isn't always easy showing someone you love him, Katharine."

I thought of Emily.

"I know," I said.

# 18

# Breaking through

Snow and December arrived together that year. The Christmas before last, my parents had gone to Calgary to visit Marilyn and, at the last minute, I'd come out in chickenpox. Emily's mother rushed to the rescue and I spent the holiday at the Blairs'.

Until then, the way we spent Christmas had not bothered me. Dad was never jovial, but we had a tree and we gave gifts. (The cards were always in Mother's writing.) It was a bit tense, a time to get through, but fun too. Everybody likes presents.

The Christmas at Emily's, though, was different. It was filled with love and meaning. The next year, ours seemed empty in a new way.

Even the gifts did not make it real.

This time, I wished we didn't have to bother. I fought to forget those days at the Blairs'. I couldn't. Emily was with me at every turn. She had given me a book of her own poems that Christmas. One of them was called "To Kate." The last verse read:

Then you came banging in my life
And all I wished came true.
I have the friend I dreamed about—
You.

I did not need to look it up to remember. I knew each word.

Then the nights of Chanukah came. I knew when. Susannah told me one day when she and I met, walking in the park in the new soft snow. She was bright with excitement. They were going to light the last candle that very evening.

"They're tippy, the candles," she explained. By now, Susannah knew that there were many things I did not know. "Daddy keeps worrying that we're going to set the house on fire, Kate. But I do love lighted candles. They look almost alive, don't they?"

I nodded.

That night, I walked around to Leigh Crescent. I kept telling myself I wouldn't see anything and I was crazy. I kept going. I stopped across the street from their window.

You would have thought they knew I was

there, except there was no way they could have known. I was careful to keep back out of sight. Still I'd only been out there a couple of minutes when Mrs. Rosenthal came to the window and then the rest—Sheila, Susannah, Dr. Rosenthal, and a tall, black-haired boy.

The magnificent brother, I thought.

Even Sheila looked beautiful from where I was standing. The candles shone out one by one like small brave stars. I remembered what I'd read about this festival, about the fight, so long ago, for freedom to worship the one invisible God.

I swallowed, took a last look, and started home.

They looked so all together, that family. I knew there were tensions there too. I'd seen them myself. I thought back to that awful morning when Sheila had cramps. My father had never treated me that way. Never.

But we weren't one family that way either.

Christmas came and went. It wasn't so bad. The new year began. I spent a lot of time by myself.

I watched Emily, though. I kept expecting to see her with Carol Davidson. I've always liked Carol myself—and she was in Emily's homeroom now. But I did not see them together. Emily seemed to be alone mostly too.

We spoke in the hall, of course. Once in

awhile, we'd even say something like "Gee, we hardly ever see each other any more!" Then we'd wait for things to change. Nothing did.

I couldn't bear to read some of my poems now. I had written a lot about friendship when I was sure ours would last for always. There was one queer little one that tugged at me. You wouldn't have guessed it would, from the first few lines.

### Clothes

I like new clothes.
They seem brighter, smoother, shinier.
I move carefully in them.
I remember to hang them up.
I feel taller in them and prettier.
And I don't climb over barbed-wire fences.

I like old clothes too.
I don't think about them much.
They are part of me—going where I go,
Doing whatever I feel like doing.
They don't expect me to be so tall;
They know my size exactly.

You know, it's a funny thing—
Friends are like clothes.

Maybe that was it. Maybe I hadn't thought about being friends enough. Maybe I had taken too much for granted.

But I didn't know how to go back and undo the wrong.

I went on helping in the store and reading and thinking about things and hoping I'd run into Susannah and waiting for a miracle that never happened.

One morning Sheila let me help her with her math. She helped me first. It was kind of sneaky really—and funny. We weren't friends.

Yet she wasn't "the only other Jewish kid in my class" any longer. She was turning into herself, Sheila Rosenthal, sister of Susannah, sister of Marc. Dumb Sheila who was maybe as lonely as I was. Maybe not though. I don't think she'd ever had an Emily.

In March, the phone call came. Mother answered.

"Jon," she said, the receiver clenched in her hand, "it's your sister."

Dad was at the telephone in two strides.

"Abby," he said, "what is it?"

He listened. His eyes widened. His face seemed to go gray.

"Thank you for calling," he said formally. "I'll come right away. No, Abby. I will come. It doesn't matter now. Yes, I'll come by myself. Yes. Goodbye, Abby."

He hung up. He looked at the two of us as though he did not know us.

"My father is dead," he said dully. "He had a stroke this afternoon."

He turned and started down the hall toward their bedroom. Mother took a step after him.

"No!" he half-shouted. "Leave me. Leave me alone!"

She stood where she was. He took another step, another.

Then my mother just ran after him.

"Slim," she cried out. "Oh, Slim!"

I can't tell you how she said it. Her voice was all in little pieces. He stopped. He sort of glared right through her. But she wouldn't leave it that way. She grabbed hold of both his shoulders and pulled him to her. If she said anything else, I don't remember. Her face was covered with tears.

"Come with me, April," he said then, holding onto her. "Come with me."

What they said made sense, I guess, but it wasn't what they said. It was their love. I could see the hurt she had seen. He was full of hurting. She just wouldn't leave him alone with it. She went right in and hurt with him.

They went into their room and closed the door. I knew they wouldn't think of me. They have always been a pair, and while I'm theirs and they love me and all that, I'm not part of that pair. It's the difference between us and the Rosenthals, I think.

I went and got my jacket. I walked quickly up one street and across three. It wasn't so far. Not far enough to have been between us all this time.

Emily came to the door herself. I was glad. I didn't want anyone else to see me, not right then.

"Kate . . ." she said, and waited, not knowing why I had come.

"Emily," I said, putting all of myself I could into every word. "I never met anybody I like better than you. Although you are often a trial to me, I believe we can still be friends when we are old, old ladies in wheelchairs."

"Oh, Kate, you idiot!" Emily cried.

"Let's be friends again, Emily," I said, as though I were Susannah's size.

"Yes, please," Emily said. "Although you're a trial to me too."

Then I knew why Mother hadn't said more to Dad. There were no words that could get past the joy, the tears, the love, that crowded into my throat.

# 19

# Beginning

So I came to the deciding place—and the decision was there waiting for me. All the thinking, all the remembering were not needed. Or were they? I only know that I knew what came next, all at once, and that was what mattered.

In April, a year after I'd found Susannah out skipping, I went to the synagogue. I told Mother ahead of time. I had to. I couldn't tell Dad. He had never spoken again of taking me.

Mother sat at the kitchen table and looked up at me. Her face wore the strangest expression. Wistful? I'm not sure. But suddenly, I said,

"Would you come with me? I'm scared really. I don't know what to do when I get there."

She sat a moment silently, and then she shook her head.

"I would like to, Kate," she said quietly, "but I should have gone over twenty years ago. Marriage is such a complicated thing. You don't know, when you're twenty, that you are marrying a man's whole life, not just an individual. He told me he didn't want to go. It was easiest to believe him. But I should have looked deeper. Perhaps I could have learned. Perhaps I still can. But if I ever do, Kate, it will have to be with your father. It isn't fair to you, but that is the way it is."

I nodded. I wanted to weep but I didn't. April does not welcome weeping.

"Elsa could take you," she offered. "I'll call her, if you like."

I was tempted. But there was Sheila. And I was not that sure. I wanted to praise God who had been with me—but I had to go my way. I wasn't a Rosenthal.

I ran back to my room for one last moment. It was still there on my dresser. Bess's picture. Aunt Abigail had let Dad have two of them and he had given this one to me. She wasn't yet married when the picture was taken. It was faded and small but you could see something of her real self in it. And I did have her eyes.

"And her chin," Mother said, when she saw it.

"I'm going now," I half-whispered to the picture of Bess.

For Bess was one of my reasons for going. Bess had loved God. Bess and Susannah—and Emily too, although she worshipped in the Presbyterian Church. They all had a steadfastness. I wanted to share it and to say thank you for them.

But you already do that here at home, a voice within argued.

I had no answer. I simply knew I had made up my mind. Or I had found my mind made up. I put down the picture and left the house.

I set out just before dusk. I knew exactly where it was. I'd walked past it often enough. I already knew the rabbi even. He'd been on the lawn one day and we'd talked—just about how cold March was and didn't I think young people should dress more warmly. He sounded a bit fossily, but I liked him. I wondered if he knew who I was. I didn't tell him.

I walked more and more slowly as I got close to the synagogue. I had on my best clothes. I hadn't worn a hat. I was pretty sure that much was all right.

"'The Lord is my shepherd,'" I muttered, bolstering my courage.

But what did I know of shepherds? I needed something else. A friend. "An ever-present help in time of trouble." Wasn't there something like that?

I was there. I stood still and looked. I saw Jackie Bernstein's father. I was on the far side of the street. I could yet walk away. Nobody would know but Mother, and she wouldn't tell.

Mr. Bernstein went in. Some people I'd never seen before followed. Then more strangers. Then the Rosenthals.

"Kate!" Susannah called joyously.

Trust Susannah! For once, I wished she and I weren't fast friends, after all.

And yet, she was one of the reasons I wanted to praise Him.

"Come on, Susan," her father said.

He glanced over at me. Then he stopped and watched me. I stood too. He started to turn away; then he turned back and began to cross the street.

"Wait a minute," he said to the others.

I shrank back—but, all at once, he smiled and turned around and went back to his family. At the same moment, a hand closed on my shoulder.

"All right, daughter," my father said, very softly. "But just one moment, before we go in.

I said nothing. I could not believe he had come.

"The answers are not all in there, Katharine," he said.

He was still speaking quietly but his voice was urgent too, as though he were giving me the most important thing he had—the meaning within his life.

"You must not go in thinking everything will be solved for you. It isn't that easy. God leaves so much for us to do."

I thought of my finally going to Emily.

"I know that," I said. "I do, really."

"All right. But you'll need to be brave, and you'll need to be . . . I guess you'll just need to be you," he said. "Come."

We started across the street.

"Are you afraid?" he asked.

I nodded.

"So am I, Katharine," he said. "It's a good way to be. It's the beginning of reverence maybe."

"How did you guess—?" I began.

I knew, though. He smiled, seeing I knew.

"Your mother told me," he said, putting it into words between us. "She sent me, Kate, but I did want to come."

Then we went in together.

# About the Author

Jean Little has published numerous popular and award-winning picture books and young adult fiction titles, including *From Anna*, *Hey World Here I Am!*, *Revenge of the Small Small* and *Mine for Keeps*. She was born in Taiwan and grew up in Ontario, receiving her degree in English and literature from the University of Toronto. She now lives near Elora, Ontario in an old stone farmhouse with her sister and four-year-old great niece, four dogs and two cats. She does her writing with a talking computer and travels extensively with her seeing eye dog, Ritz.